Liza's
Star
Wish

Diane Stevens

Liza's Star Wish

 Greenwillow Books : New York

I want to thank Jean Brody, Pat Van Rhyn, Adrienne
Lynett, Kate Rankin, Marilyn Finn, and the Cambria
Writers' Workshop—and once again, my writer-mom,
Shyrle Hacker, and my fine editor, Robin Roy, for
believing that star wishes can come true.

Library of Congress
Cataloging-in-Publication Data

Stevens, Diane.
     Liza's star wish / by Diane Stevens.
         p.   cm.
     Sequel to: Liza's blue moon.
     Summary: While unwillingly spending the summer
at her grandmother's house in Rockport, Texas,
fourteen-year-old Liza gains insights into relationships
with family and friends, old and new, and into the
effects of her younger sister's death on everyone.
     ISBN 0-688-15310-0
     [1. Family life—Texas–Fiction.
2. Interpersonal relations—Fiction.
3. Grief—Fiction.   4. Texas—Fiction.]
I. Title.
PZ7.S8439Ln 1997   [Fic]—dc21
96-46256   CIP   AC

for joe

Número Uno, always

Liza's
Star
Wish

I tried to remember the things I used to love about my grandmother. I made a mental list.

1. Stays up late
2. Doesn't look like a grandmother
3. Juggles
4.

Not one of them was true anymore. I shook cleanser into the sink and turned the water on full force.

"Don't splatter!" Mom said. She was pretending to read the paper at the kitchen table, just waiting for our conversation to be over.

"How long before she's better?" I said.

"Broken hips take a long time to heal. Mama's not as young as she used to be."

2

"That's obvious," I said.

She folded her hands and sat up straighter. "Wait till Saturday, Liza."

Her latest thing was to schedule family "confabs" for Saturdays. That meant if you felt any negative feelings between Sunday and Friday, you made a list (your "feelings homework") and saved up. She'd just read a book called *Getting Friendly with Your Feelings*. Dad and I liked it better when she used to just walk out of the room.

"I'm staying home with Dad," I said.

"Your father travels too much during the summer. Surely you understand after all we've been through."

I knew she meant my sister. It was only a year since Holly had drowned. "You don't trust me," I said.

"Of course I trust you!" She came over and put her hand on my shoulder. At least she was feeling sorry for me. I could smell the new perfume that Dad had given her that smelled like cherry vanilla ice cream. "It's just that San Antonio is a big city," she said. "Things can happen."

"What am I supposed to do in Rockport all summer?"

"We'll be a block from the beach," she said.

I reminded her how we both got sunburned and hated sand.

"Mama says there's a girl your age living next door."

"Why does she think I can't find my own friends?"

Mom closed her eyes for a second. "She worries you'll be lonely, darling. Liza, I know you think she doesn't care, but your grandmother just has a hard time showing it."

I knew she was making excuses. Mama Lacy had always loved Holly's friends and disapproved of mine.

"Just give it a try. Perhaps you can come back for a weekend or two with your father."

I could feel myself giving in. Mom's voice had this way of making you want to be a good person. "If I decide to go, I'm taking my trombone."

"That's going to be difficult in Mama's small house. We'll see. But you'll have to leave Nacho home because she won't have him scaring Porky."

I just looked at her. Nacho is my black cocker spaniel. I got him five years ago for my birthday, when I turned nine. He sleeps on the foot of my bed every night. I tell him everything.

I hated Porky even more than Nacho did. He was a balding cat with pink scabs. I knew if Mama Lacy's voice didn't scare Porky, Nacho couldn't. My grandmother's voice was so loud that you had to hold the phone away from your ear when she called. Last year she'd agreed to Dad's idea of folding a paper towel into a square and taping it over her mouthpiece.

"So what happens to Nacho while Dad's away on trips?" I figured she was dreading that question.

4

"Mama's welfare has to come first right now." She paused. "Nacho will stay at the kennel when your father's traveling. I know how much you hate that, and I don't like it either, but it won't be for too many days in a row."

Too many days! Nacho had been to the kennel only twice in his life. I knew he didn't think in days. Or hours. Each second was all he cared about. Every day had thousands and thousands of seconds. He'd have to sleep alone in a dark, cold cage, with strange beasts barking and howling all night. How would he know I was ever coming back? I felt like crying but tried not to in front of Mom. For her, crying was like flossing. You didn't do it in public.

"What about Forrest?" I said.

"You can E-mail him as often as you want since I'm taking my computer along. I'm going to try to get back to my writing this summer." Her voice sounded all light and airy now, as if she'd finished her feelings homework.

I still had a lump in my throat. Some things she didn't understand, no matter how many self-help books she read. Words weren't the main thing with Forrest and me. We talked only when there was something to talk about. Sometimes we just sat together on my roof and watched the night sky. We'd seen each other practically every day during the last year.

Mom was going on and on. ". . . and maybe after Chloe finishes her dance rehearsals, she can visit in Rockport."

"Of course she's coming," I said. "That's obvious."

"Don't raise your voice," Mom said.

I finished wiping off the counters and thought about Chloe. She'd lived on my street for our whole life until she'd moved to Houston last summer. All year we'd planned our visit, but now it had to be in Rockport, where the most exciting thing was a statue of a pink plaster crab in the town square.

Mom patted my back before she headed down the hall. She was through feeling sorry for me. Forrest believed that everyone had a pity quotient. He said it was important to recognize when yours was used up for the day.

□

I knew Mama Lacy wasn't the whole reason we were spending the summer in Rockport. I'd heard Mom say that our Willow Street house held too many memories of Holly. Mom couldn't sleep at night because she kept hearing a flute in her dreams.

Holly played flute. I play trombone. The main thing about me is I'm tall. My hair's red. It frizzes if I don't wet it and stretch it out with a kitchen fork twice a day. Holly was

6

blond and pale. She looked like the littlest angel in the Christmas pageant. She made everyone laugh, especially Mama Lacy. Holly's face glowed as if it had an opal inside. She was eleven when she died. She'll always be eleven.

At first I felt sorry for Mom. I'd bring her English muffins in bed on a tray, with a rose from her garden. I fixed most of the meals for a while. Sometimes, after dinner, when Mom would go straight to bed, Dad would turn off the TV and we'd stare at the blank screen. Then we'd talk about Holly.

"Remember the time she told me not to say anything funny until she got back from the bathroom?" I said.

Dad remembered. He liked talking about her. She almost seemed alive again when we remembered things she said and did. That was part of what I loved about Willow Street. In a way Holly *was* still there. Her room still smelled like lavender. Her swing still hung from the sycamore in the front yard. Whenever I looked at the plaid sofa in the living room, I could imagine her hand puppets, Darcinda and Robespierre, popping over the top, saying annoying things.

☐

Dad was cleaning the garage, so I went to see if he'd take pity. I'd felt closer to him during the last year than I ever had. Sometimes he came into my room late at night and sat on the foot of my bed. He wouldn't talk at all. He'd just sit there, smoking his cigarette. Maybe he figured I was asleep. Then he'd pull the cover over my shoulders and give a real light touch to the back of my head. I didn't even mind the smoke.

In the garage he had piles of stuff all over. "I'm giving these things to Goodwill," he said.

I saw Holly's flute case next to a box of her clothes. "Does Mom know you're giving all this away?"

"The less she knows right now, the better." Dad sat on a box. "Everyone says the quicker you get rid of mementos, the faster you'll get over grief. It's been a year, Liza. Time we get on with our life."

Our life? He acted as if we all had the same one. "I've already gotten on with mine," I said.

He nodded. "I hope so, hon." He kept on looking at me.

I liked the way he never asked me what I was feeling. He trusted my thoughts. Still, I wondered what "getting on with your life" really meant. All year I'd hung around home more than ever before. Mom and Dad both seemed to like it that way. After Chloe had moved, I hadn't even tried to find a new best friend.

I sat down on a huge cardboard box labeled "Shoes." Holly had always loved getting new ones. Red, pink, silver, striped, polka dot. She never gave a single pair away, even after she'd outgrown them. Once she said that by the time she was twenty, she planned to own a hundred pairs.

"Dad, I want to stay home with you this summer."

He put down the pile of clothes. "I'd like that more than anything. We've been such buddies all year."

I hated talk like that. Like a TV sitcom. It was just his warm-up to say no.

He went on. "But I'm gone so much, and your mother needs you right now."

I didn't answer. He always used his job as an excuse. He imported imitation artworks from Asia. Sometimes his fake Buddhas seemed more important than we were. Now he was only worrying about what Mom needed. What *I* needed didn't count. I started back inside to call Forrest. I'd put off telling him about Rockport because I kept wishing Mom would change her mind. Now there was no choice.

Then Dad said, "Wait a minute, Liza." He lit a cigarette. "Sit down."

I could tell by his voice it was bad news, really bad.

"I want to be straight with you about what's happening. I want you to keep on trusting me like you have all year."

I knew he meant Ms. Weller. When I was twelve, I'd found out by accident that he'd been having an affair with the woman next door. I'd never told Mom. He knew I knew, but we never talked about it. I hated remembering, even though he seemed like a different person now.

He went on. "Your mom wanted to wait to tell you later, after you spent time in Rockport, but I think it's only fair that you know now."

It was something really, really bad. Maybe they were getting a divorce. But that seemed impossible. During the last year they'd gotten along better. Sometimes Dad had made it home in time for dinner, and once he even called when he was late. I knew Ms. Weller's husband had moved back in with her next door. And Mom kept reading more self-help books about family togetherness.

"Tell me right now," I said. Someone was tying a knot inside my chest.

"Honey, your mom wants to see how you like living in Rockport."

The boxes in the garage grew big. Holly's boxes. I thought of all her shoes mixed up, mashed together. Her favorites were the tennies with red sequins that she called her Oz shoes.

"Are we all moving there? I mean, for good or something?"

"You never can tell what the future holds," he said.

Suddenly I knew exactly what the future held: a pink plaster crab.

He put out his cigarette. "Believe me, it's the last thing I'd choose, but I want your mom to be happy."

The knot inside me pulled tighter. "You want her to be happy. She wants Mama Lacy to be happy. What about me?" I kicked the box of shoes so hard my foot hurt. Then I ran inside to call Forrest.

"Can you come over right now?" I said. I knew my voice sounded shaky. My foot was still aching.

"Sure. I want you to see my new hiking boots. Let's go to Brackenridge on Sunday."

"Hiking? You can't stand walking to my house," I said. Forrest was planning to be a foot doctor, but he seldom actually used his feet.

In thirty minutes he arrived in his orthopedic hiking boots. His size twelve looked huge with the purple stripes. "Liza, these are the first shoes I've ever had where my feet feel like running. It's like they have pride in themselves."

"Running?" Forrest moved almost as slow as Mama Lacy, but I didn't discourage him. He was the tallest guy I knew, with the biggest feet. People always assumed he was a jock.

It was already dark when we climbed out my window onto the roof. I always did my best thinking up there. The first star seemed especially close. I made a wish: that by the end of summer we'd come back home forever to Willow Street. *Forever.*

Forrest was still talking about running, something about early-morning workouts and wanting me to time him. I knew I had to say it.

"Forrest, I'm going away."

He looked at me. "On vacation?"

"Mom calls it that. We're going to Rockport to take care of my grandmother, who broke her hip."

"The one with the loud voice who burps?"

I nodded.

"But it's not forever," Forrest said. He took my hand.

Forever. Then I almost said it. *I might not be coming back. We're moving.* But something stopped me. Maybe he wouldn't write me all summer if he thought I was leaving for good. Maybe he'd want to "get on with *his* life." I'd just be the tall redhead with the trombone, who used to live on Willow Street.

I wasn't crying, but I had a lump in my throat the size of an apricot. I felt too mad to cry. Mad at Mom for wanting to go. Mad at Dad for letting her. Mad at Mama Lacy for breaking her hip. Even mad at Holly for dying.

Forrest said, "Liza, you're the only girl I've ever really talked to, including my mother."

12

I looked at him, but he was watching the sky. I tried to memorize his exact words so I wouldn't forget. I knew he cared, but he'd never said it aloud. I could feel tears starting. I guess he noticed because he gave me his handkerchief.

"I didn't know you had monogrammed handkerchiefs," I said.

"Got them for Christmas from my mother. That's how well she knows me. Can you believe monogrammed handkerchiefs? That's why I need you."

When Forrest said he needed me, I started to cry, full force. My shoulders shook, and my chest felt as if the knot had come loose. I hadn't cried in front of him before, even after Holly died. His handkerchief was getting all wrinkled.

He put his arm around me and said, "Liza, look at the moon. It's all alone up there."

He was right. The sky was black. Funny how one star can be so bright, then next time you look it's gone. "I made a wish on the first star," I said, "but where did it go?"

He paused. "Liza, I think you wished on an airplane." Then he took off his glasses and kissed me. It was the best kiss so far. He closed his eyes. I didn't. I wanted to remember everything. I wanted to remember the way Forrest smelled like cloves. I wanted to remember how his nose felt cold as an ice cube and how his right earlobe looked pink and soft, like Play-Doh.

My whole body felt like a helium balloon, ready to float straight up. I looked at the sky. The fog had closed in.

Finally I said, "Going away is worse than dying. Everyone forgets you."

Forrest pressed my hand and said, "I won't. Hey, where did the moon go?"

"Maybe it had to go to Rockport," I said.

chapter 2

"Be quiet, Liza! Mama Lacy's sleeping."

"Go ask your grandmother if she's hungry!"

"She's yelling for something. Go see what she wants!"

I did what Mom said, but Mama Lacy never once said thank you. Mom said some people just didn't have those words in their vocabulary. She said it wasn't Mama Lacy's fault. Nothing was ever Mama Lacy's fault.

I hated the wheelchair. It barely fitted through the bathroom door. I had to remember to put the brakes on both sides before I lifted Mama Lacy onto the toilet. Once I forgot the brakes. She started rolling and yelling at me at the same time, "Elizabeth Jane, I'll fall. I'll fall!"

Sometimes I almost wished she would.

□

Everything in Rockport smelled like shrimp, especially the bathtub. Mama Lacy said Daddy Jake used to come home from his fishing trips with buckets of shrimp and haul them with ice into the bathroom. He'd say, "Who needs a freezer when you got a good tub?"

Daddy Jake was a plumber, so he respected bathtubs more than the average person. Now he lived at a retirement home called Moonhaven. Mama Lacy said she'd taken care of him long enough. He wasn't helpless, but his feet hurt when he walked because of bad circulation from diabetes.

He used to read to me on the front porch, not kids' books, just whatever bird book he happened to be reading. He said there was no such thing as kids' books because there was no such thing as kids. I never felt like a kid when I was with Daddy Jake.

I wanted Mom to take me to see him at Moonhaven as soon as we arrived in Rockport, but Mama Lacy said, "Your mother's too exhausted, Liza!" Her voice sounded like a foghorn. She'd been a high school gym teacher and spent her life yelling at girls who couldn't serve a volleyball.

Mom didn't object. She was exhausted a lot. Mama Lacy said it was part of Mom's depression. I had to be quiet in the afternoons so Mom could sleep. I had to be quiet in the evenings so Mama Lacy could sleep.

The only good thing about the shrimp house was my room in the roof. The ceilings were so slanted you had to duck your head, unless you were right in the middle. I loved living in a roof, even though my room was furnished with just two cots, one under each window, no rug or dresser or chair. Mom let me keep her computer in my room because she didn't feel like writing yet, but the only place for it was on the bare floor. Mama Lacy said too much comfort made you "a softy."

She called the skinny windows in the roof dormer windows. I could see out one dormer window across Raht Street to a pink house with lime green shutters and a red statue of the Virgin on the front porch. Mama Lacy said it was tacky, but I thought it was great. Like the colors from the game Candy Land that Holly and I used to play when we were little.

Through the other dormer window I could see the pier and the lighthouse that blinked every eight seconds. I liked knowing it was blinking even while I slept. Holly used to love my stories about lone survivors at sea, marooned in the fog. We imagined we were guiding them home.

□

Mom made supper. Pork was the main thing Mama Lacy liked. Baked potatoes, cabbage, and pork. Mom wasn't eating her potato, just drinking iced tea in tiny sips and daydreaming. I figured she thought about Holly most at suppertime. I thought about her then, too, but I didn't miss the way she'd flipped food off her fork at me when no one was looking.

"It's nice to be home again," Mom said, glancing around the room. Her words didn't match her face.

The sofa was covered with Dad's scratchy navy blanket, which Mama Lacy took off only for special company. Daddy Jake said she might remove it for five minutes if the Pope came to visit. I knew if I ever had a house of my own, it would smell like chocolate chip cookies and have French lace curtains like Chloe's.

"I thought home was San Antonio," I said.

Mama Lacy picked up her cat, Porky, and put him in her lap. "Home is where you make it."

I took a bite of dry pork. I missed good food. At home Mom let me cook, but Mama Lacy didn't like my messing up her kitchen. I figured Forrest was swimming right now at the Willow Street pool. I loved the time just before dark when the underwater lights came on and made stars on the water.

"I know it's not the same for you as me, Liza," Mom said, "but the sea air will be good for both of us. It's healing."

"Healing" was one of Mom's new words. She said that feelings took even longer to heal than broken bones. I remembered Holly pulling a scab off her knee and watching it bleed.

Mom hadn't eaten much. Mama Lacy traded plates with her, then glopped Miracle Whip onto the potato and took a bite. She always said Miracle Whip perked up everything. I wished it would perk up Mom.

"Elizabeth Jane?" Mama Lacy said. "There's a girl next door named Jennifer Wells whose father's on the city council. She's the perfect friend for you. Go knock on her door."

I couldn't stand the thought of knocking on a door to find a friend. I figured a friend was like sleep. It just happened.

Besides, why make friends when you're not planning to stay? I kept my suitcase open on the bedroom floor, with my clothes stacked inside. My trombone case sat there, too, but I hadn't opened it yet. Mama Lacy hated loud things, except her own voice.

She was looking at me, taking short breaths, her hand on her chest. That meant palpitations. Sometimes she couldn't say a whole sentence at once because she didn't have enough air. "I think you should go straight over next door . . ."

I nodded and started clearing. After I'd done the dishes, I headed out.

Mama Lacy yelled after me, "Don't trip on the welcome mat!"

When she couldn't think of good advice, she gave bad advice. I cut across the grass, past her dead rosebushes; she used to win prizes for her roses at the garden show. They had all kinds of great names, like First Love and Brandy and Hula Girl and Snowfire. After Holly, she'd just let them all die.

I didn't even look at Jennifer's gray house. No one fun could live in a house that gray. I knew Mama Lacy didn't like my friends at home. Once when she was visiting, she caught me and Chloe on the roof smoking Dad's cigars. Later she told me that friends were food for the soul and that I existed on junk food. Chloe said her feelings for Mama Lacy were mutual.

I headed for the beach barefoot. The sidewalk burned my feet. Forrest believed feet were braver than any other part of the body, so I wanted to test how much pain my brave feet could stand.

I stood on the dock and watched the seagulls squawk and dive. An Asian family got off a fishing boat and covered it with canvas. They all were talking at once as they walked up the beach with their arms around one another. In a family like that you wouldn't have to keep quiet for someone who was always sleeping. I watched them until they were out of sight.

Then I looked up the beach toward the lighthouse. When Holly was little, she'd never walk there with me because she imagined the meanest man in the world lived inside with the meanest woman in the world. She said someday they would have hundreds of mean children. "It would serve them both right," she said. She believed justice prevailed.

I decided against going to the lighthouse. It was lonely after dark. I tried to find the first star but couldn't even find the moon through the fog. Like somebody had erased it. When I got back to the house, I looked across the street and saw a girl wearing Rollerblades, sitting on the Candy Land front porch. You'd *have* to be fun if you lived there. I wanted to go over, but I hate that part before you know someone.

When I first met Chloe, she didn't tell me that she was hard-of-hearing. She didn't answer when I asked her things. For a long time I figured she didn't want to be my friend.

I waved at the Rollerblade girl, and she waved back. Maybe I'd have more nerve tomorrow.

Then I went inside. I could smell Mama Lacy's gardenia perfume, which she only wore when she went out. I remembered they'd gone to a meeting at the church. I loved having the house to myself. I headed for the kitchen and rooted around for something, but all I could find were graham crackers that bent instead of crunched. Mama Lacy always said she didn't care if they got stale because she soaked them in hot Ovaltine, anyhow, and ate them with a spoon.

I wanted to make cookies, but I knew after one day of humidity they'd turn into sponges. I found a box of raisins, probably a hundred years old, and ate a handful as I wandered past the pantry and saw Mama Lacy's bedroom door, closed like always. I knew I wasn't supposed to go in. She said it was absolutely off-limits, except to Mom. I wondered what she was hiding in there that was so special.

I opened the door. I smelled Clorox. She'd bleached her chenille bedspread so many times that now it was just rows of white bumps, like old popcorn.

I didn't turn on the light, but the room was partly lit from the hall. Her dresser was covered with photos, about twenty, in silver frames. All of them were of Holly: Holly in her leotard; Holly playing her flute in the talent show; Holly with Mama Lacy beside the Christmas tree.

I saw one tiny photo of me at the back of the dresser. I was standing on a stage, receiving the district spelling bee award I'd won in fifth grade. I was squinting, with my mouth wide open and braces glowing, my hair puffed out like cotton candy. Why did she choose my all-time ugliest picture for her dresser?

I could smell lavender. I opened the top drawer and saw a stack of letters tied with pink ribbon and recognized Holly's handwriting. From the time she was little, she always wrote to Mama Lacy. I only wrote when Mom told me to. Then I saw Holly's lavender sachets. I closed the drawer fast and stood there feeling cold all over.

I wanted to push all the pictures onto the floor. Did Mama Lacy think she was the only one who missed her? Then I said the worst thing out loud. "If you'd just die, Mama Lacy, we could go home!" I couldn't believe I'd said it.

Then I could hear Holly saying, "Liza, you know what? You don't really mean that!"

I couldn't tell if I felt hungry or sick. I turned my mug shot facedown on her dresser, then went upstairs and changed into my yellow nightshirt before I remembered Mama Lacy had given it to me for Christmas. Chloe had said, "That's urine yellow, Liza, if I ever saw it."

I missed Chlo so much, even though it had been a whole year since she'd moved. We'd talked on the phone once a week since she'd left, but that wasn't the same. I knew she couldn't hear everything I said and only pretended. She was embarrassed about being hard-of-hearing, even around me.

In fourth grade we'd made a pact to draw a tiny ruby heart with a Magic Marker on the palms of our right hands every morning before school. We vowed never to tell anyone what the heart meant: *Forever Together*. Whenever we'd see each other in the hall between classes, we'd flash our right palms and whisper, "Heart/heart."

Last summer Chlo's parents announced they were getting a divorce and moving to separate houses in Houston. I couldn't believe it; they were the perfect couple. Even her mom's name was the perfect name: Gabrielle. But Chloe said her parents weren't as perfect as they seemed. She was mad about the divorce and said she'd rather not talk about it. She never talked about bad stuff that happened to her.

Chloe and I had watched the moving van drive off with all their stuff. Then I'd helped pack the trunk of their Honda while her poodle, Lilac, peered at me from the backseat. I loved Lilac second best to Nacho.

Finally I'd hugged Chloe good-bye. Gabrielle was already behind the wheel, with the motor running, but Chloe and I held on to each other and couldn't let go. Neither of us said a word. Then Chloe got in the front and didn't roll her window down because she could never hear, anyhow, when the motor was running. She just put her right palm up against the car window and smiled at me.

"Heart/heart," I whispered. I knew she could read my lips.

Then all I could see was the green Honda, disappearing down Willow Street, forever.

24

Summer came all at once the day Chlo left. One day it was bluebonnet weather, then just sopping heat. The air conditioner clicked on and off all night, waking me up. I'd lie there, gazing at the sparkles on the plaster ceiling. They looked like stars, but you couldn't wish on them. Holly used to hate the sparkles. She said they were like God's eyes, watching her every move.

☐

I took off the yellow nightshirt and put on the blue one Dad had given me. It had stars and planets all over it. I gazed toward the lighthouse and counted eight seconds. Nothing. The fog had closed in.

I reached into the bottom of my suitcase and got out the tissue-wrapped photo of Chloe and me. We'd had it taken at Six Flags two summers ago. We were dressed in old-fashioned clothes to make us look older. Now I couldn't believe how young we looked then. I put the photo back in the suitcase because there was no place to display it, then turned on the computer to E-mail Forrest. He'd come up with our gender-correct E-mail addresses before I left home.

E-male
I'm sorry I didn't get to stop by again before I left. Mom insisted we get an early start. My life is not a priority these days.

25

If you knew what I wished for Mama Lacy, you'd probably change your mind about me.
E-female

I climbed onto my cot and put my pillow against my legs, so it would feel like Nacho. Wherever he was sleeping, he was probably shivering without me there beside him. I wished *I* were shivering. Mama Lacy always turned the air-conditioning off at night to save money. She said the sea breeze was plenty cool if I just opened my window, but nothing was ever cool in Rockport.

I heard the wheelchair squeaking as Mama Lacy and Mom came in downstairs. I closed my eyes. "Look what you're missing, Holl!" I said out loud. I could hear bathwater running. I smelled shrimp.

The girl with the Rollerblades sat on her porch. Even though she looked a lot younger, I made myself go over. Forrest always said it was character building to do things you didn't want to do.

She was reading a Spanish comic book. *"Buenas tardes. I'm Paz,"* she said.

Her name rhymed with Oz. I thought of Holly's Oz shoes. "I'm Liza," I said. I decided to try my Spanish. I asked her if it was hard to Rollerblade. I didn't know the word for "Rollerblade," so I pointed to her feet. She told me to speak English because she could understand everything but felt shy to speak it with some people. I figured I wasn't one of them.

"I wear them to be tall," she said, standing up.

"Why do you want to be tall? People take care of you if you're small."

"I have almost twelve years, but no one believes."

She barely came to my shoulder and was really skinny. She looked about eight. She had Band-Aids on her knees, and her hair was long and wavy, not big like mine. She wore a print sundress with green-and-white-striped elephants. Paz said her mother made all her clothes. She wrinkled her nose as though she hated the idea.

She told me to wait, then skated on the path to her back-yard. She returned with a goat loping along behind. "Eliza, this is Hector. He is more tall than many goats because I give him buttered popcorn and Coke."

Paz said Hector kept their front grass short so they never had to mow it. She was training him not to eat the roses by feeding him a sardine every time he disobeyed. "Sardines give goats heartburn," she said. Then she asked where I'd moved from.

"San Antonio. It's not a move, though. Just a visit." I told her how I called her house Candy Land. "It looks like it's made out of gumdrops,"

She said she liked it, too. "Everything here in Texas I like," she said, "especially hamburgers. Better than Guada-lajara."

"How long have you lived here?"

"Almost two years we are here. Every month we go to Houston. I have shots there to make me grow tall. In Mexico they don't have the tall shots."

"Don't you miss home?"

Paz shrugged. "I only miss two things in Mexico: my father and my rabbit, Presto." She said Presto grew twice as fast as most rabbits because she raised him on eggplant. She said she would write a book someday on what animals should eat. She tied Hector to the front porch rail and then started to skate down the sidewalk. I jogged along.

"I wish I had Rollerblades," I said. "My mom says they're dangerous. She thinks everything's dangerous."

"You can one day borrow mine. I have big feet. See? That means I am already growing tall like you."

"My boyfriend, Forrest, believes that big feet mean you have a big brain. He wants to be a foot doctor," I said. It was the first time ever that I'd called Forrest my boyfriend.

We got to the corner and turned around. Paz said she didn't want to stay away from Hector too long because he hadn't been well.

"I've been feeling sort of sick, too," I said. I didn't tell her I meant homesick. I'd been missing Forrest. He hadn't answered my E-mail.

"The thing for goat sinus is broccoli." She planned to be an animal doctor when she grew up, she said.

"It's called a veterinarian. Forrest thinks it's a weird word because it has two *e*'s, two *a*'s, two *r*'s, two *i*'s, and two *n*'s."

She asked me to write it down later, so she could send it in a letter to her father.

"Where is he?"

"In Mexico. One day he comes, but not yet. He stays in Guadalajara, making churches with stone." Then she asked me what I wanted to be when I grew up.

"Maybe a writer," I said. I felt fake when I said it because I hadn't written a poem since Holly.

"You must come tonight." She said her brother taught dancing every Friday at the pier. "Salsa," she said. "You have a brother?"

"No, I used to have a sister, but she died." My voice sounded distant, like someone else's. I was glad Paz didn't ask questions or say she was sorry. "Sorry" was like "bless you" when you sneezed. I hated it.

When we got back to her house, she said she'd see me at the pier at eight. I patted Hector.

When I opened the front door, I saw Mama Lacy watching TV. She liked reruns of *To Tell the Truth* and said she knew she'd have been accepted as a contestant because she could lie better than anyone. Once I asked why she thought she could lie better than most people. She said you got a lot of practice by the time you were seventy-two. "There are things more important than the truth," she said. She wouldn't say what things.

Now she was in a good mood. "My name is Thelma Lacy, and I used to own the Houdini Museum in New York." Then she smiled with her new teeth, which were all the same size, like eggs in a carton.

I loved it when Mama Lacy played games. When I was little, she used to play gin rummy with me on the porch while Holly napped. When Holly grew up and got cuter, Mama Lacy quit gin rummy.

"All in learning to keep a poker face," she said. "Jake always said I had a good one."

"You don't look a bit like you own a museum," I said.

She laughed. "Jake's the one who belongs in a museum."

I hated when she said things like that about my grandfather. "Do you miss having him home?"

She sniffled. "Always had his head under someone's sink. Carried a plunger everywhere in case he needed to make a house call."

"What's that got to do with anything?"

She shook her head. "He wore a work shirt that read, 'I can drain anything.' Said he'd never go in the bay because he wouldn't swim in anything he couldn't drain. Folks laughed at Jake Lacy." She started to wheel herself out of the room. I almost tapped her on the back so she'd stay, but she didn't have the kind of back you could tap.

"Can't help his body gave up on him same time I did,"
she said. Her words snapped like bites of celery.

"Still, you must miss him," I said.

She called out from the kitchen, "What's the good of
missing someone when they're gone?"

I thought about what she'd said. She was right. There
was no use.

☐

I figured Mom would be glad to hear I'd found a friend.
At dinner I told her.

"Her name's Paz. She's really small for her age. She
says her family moved here from Mexico so she could get
shots to make her taller. Is there such a thing?"

Mom nodded. "Growth hormones, I suppose."

"Why do they sneak across the border for our doctors?"
Mama Lacy said. "Don't they have their own?"

I knew she was just mad because we were having shrimp
for dinner. I looked at Mom. "I'm going to a dance with
Paz at the pier tonight."

Mom said, "Uh-huh," and sipped her tea.

Mama Lacy said, "That pier's the last place for you. The
bad element's taking over. You can find better things to do
with your time than dancing." She moved the salt shaker

about an inch, then moved it back again. I hated the way she moved things around on the table for no reason.

"What's better to do with my time? At least I don't end out watching quiz shows."

"End up. Watch your grammar. What I do with my time is my business, Elizabeth Jane." She sipped her beer.

Mom pushed her chair back from the table. "Please," she said, "not today."

No one talked much until we finished dinner. Mom was humming to herself. I hadn't heard her hum in a while. Maybe that meant she was happy in Rockport. What if she'd already made the decision about moving for good and was just afraid to tell me? She talked to Dad on the phone a lot, but always in a low voice. Every time I asked her what was going to happen, she said, "We'll see."

I began loading the dishwasher. I'd just sneak out when no one was around. Mom hadn't exactly said no. She was putting the food away and wiping the table.

"Did you go knock on Jennifer's door yet?" Mama Lacy said. "She's smart like you are. I think you two might hit it off."

"She wasn't home," I lied. I finished washing the pots and told Mom I was going upstairs to read.

☐

I checked my E-mail.

"You've got mail!" I loved that computer voice. It was my best friend in Rockport.

> E-female
> It's sad not to feel like a priority, but it's a good word just the same. Four vowels. Don't worry about wishing bad things for your grandmother. Wishes have no basis in reality. Same with astrology and fortune cookies. It's magic. Only for people who fear the unknown. The reason I haven't been near the computer is that my mother decided that because I'm an Aquarius, I have a natural "athletic bent." Can you believe that? She signed me up for a weight-lifting class, but I couldn't carry the box of weights from the department store to the car, so we had to get them delivered for $25. She's still mad. I'll write more later. I have to go lift. Things aren't the same.
> E-male

Forrest was right. Things weren't the same. As soon as you got used to something, it changed.

☐

I could hear Mom talking to Dad on the kitchen phone. I knew he'd ask to talk to me. I hated those conversations because I could never tell him anything real. Mama Lacy just sat there listening. He was coming down in two weeks, so at least I'd get to go back home soon for a visit. Only fifteen days till I'd see Forrest and Nacho.

I had no trouble sneaking out the back door. No one had forbidden me to go, anyway. I got to the pier on time and saw about a dozen kids there. The guys wore white, starched shirts and dark pants. Forrest never wore a starched shirt, only white T-shirts with no words on them. He always said reading was a serious choice and you shouldn't have it thrust upon you every time you glanced at someone's chest.

Most of the girls were dressed up and had ribbons or barrettes in their hair. I was wearing jeans and my "Don't Mess with Texas" T-shirt. My hair had already kinked for the night. I felt like turning around and going back, but it was too early and too hot and too lonely to sleep. Then I spotted Paz, who seemed really short without her Rollerblades. I told her she smelled like limes.

"That is *limón* hair spray," she said. "*Limón* is always making the hair curl." She pointed to a guy in a black shirt who was setting up speakers for music. "He is my brother, Beto," she said.

She took my hand. Hers was tiny, with short nails polished in fluorescent pink. "Come, Eliza." She led me over to the group and told them I was new in town.

"I'm just visiting," I said.

Everyone was Mexican but me. Still, no one seemed to

mind. I was sorry that most of them spoke English because I'd wanted to practice my Spanish.

"My brother has sixteen years and sometimes plays guitar," she said. Beto shook my hand in a formal way, bowing his head. He looked older than sixteen and held his chin high, as if he were proud of something besides himself.

"My name is Beto Castillo," he said. His name sounded round and curly.

"Mine's Eliza," I said, deciding on Paz's version.

He wore shiny black shoes, not tennies, and had more hair on his head than most guys, dark and straight and shiny like on a shampoo ad. I wished I'd forked mine out flatter.

Fast music played, and everyone seemed to know who their partners were. Beto held out his hand. "I will dance with you tonight, if you don't mind?" His words sounded clipped and perfect. He said he'd studied English from audiotapes that his uncle had sent him when he was in Mexico.

He showed me the salsa step. It wasn't hard, but I kept watching his shiny shoes and getting messed up. I knew he'd rather be dancing with someone who already knew how. Like Chloe.

"You must relax your shoulders," Beto said. I figured he was already sorry he'd asked me. He moved his shoulders up and down and told me to do the same. Afterward I felt more relaxed. I could see the bay glistening below from the string of lights on the pier. The music rose in the air, then came back down as if it didn't want to leave.

I couldn't talk and dance at the same time, so I just danced, and Beto let me know when he wanted to turn by pressing his hand on my waist. It felt like the way I played my trombone when I knew the notes really well. I'd just barely touch the slide.

I remembered how at the Valentine Dance, Forrest had stepped on my foot and apologized about fifty times, pausing now and then to check us for foot damage.

I could see Beto's face clearly because we were under the spotlight. His eyes were the color of dark chocolate.

When the music stopped, I said, "Do you miss home?"

"I miss my father," he said.

"Why doesn't he come to Texas?"

He paused. "We are here only for some months for my sister's treatment. Then we return. My father is a stone-mason and must work in Guadalajara."

The music started again, this time a waltz. I'd already learned the box step from Chloe. Beto held out his hand and grasped me tighter around the waist, turning as we waltzed. The lights on the pier made reflections in the water like colored stars.

"You are learning fast, Eliza," he said.

I could tell I was getting better. Paz danced with her

partner, who seemed twice as tall as she was, but she kept up fine, even without Rollerblades.

Finally the music stopped for the night. Beto took his hand from my waist. I could see tiny sparks in the air all around us.

"Lightflies," he said.

"You mean fireflies."

He smiled. We said good night.

Paz and I walked home together while Beto stayed behind to straighten up. I could almost hear the waltzes floating back down from the sky. I saw bunches of stars, but I could never name the constellations without Forrest.

We turned the corner onto Raht Street. The lights were already out at Jennifer Wells's. "Do you know her?" I said, pointing to the gray house.

Paz shook her head. "Miss Crab Queen."

"What?"

"The parade," Paz said. "Last year Jennifer was picked to wear the crab crown."

"Do you like her?"

Paz shrugged.

"You'll love my best friend, Chloe," I said. "She'll be here soon." I wondered if Paz would love her. Not everyone did at first. When Chloe met new kids, she didn't talk at all or else she talked too much. About herself. I knew it

38

was because she couldn't hear. Some kids at school thought she was a snob; a few even told her so. She said that was their problem, not hers, but once Gabrielle told me that Chloe cried a lot at night about how unfair it was to be born hard-of-hearing.

Paz asked me over the next day to help her mother make tortillas.

"I'll come over for a while before we go visit my grandfather," I said. "He's great. He loves birds and knows tons about them."

"Birds are hating birdseed," she said, "and liking cocoa."

"How do you know?"

"Of course I give them some and watch them chirp loud and fly high. Tell your grandfather." Then she asked me to her birthday party. "Twelve is the year I grow tall." Paz kept her nose tilted as she walked, as if she were smelling something great. She ran up her walk and waved from the porch, where Hector was sleeping on the doormat.

c h a p t e r 4

I put on my shorts and Emily Dickinson T-shirt and went downstairs. Mama Lacy was scraping her burned toast. She always burned it first so she could scrape it. She said it was the toaster's fault, but even after Dad had given her a new one for Christmas, nothing changed. Dad said some grandmothers liked knitting and crocheting, but Mama Lacy liked burning and scraping. I slipped out the door before she could give me advice.

I went around to Paz's backyard so I could see Hector, who was eating a bowl of Cheerios. Paz opened the door and motioned me into the kitchen, which smelled like fresh bread. Someone was kneading dough on a cutting board.

"This is my mother," Paz said, holding out her hand as if she were introducing Miss America. When her mother turned and smiled at me, I could see why. She looked like one of the flamenco dancers that I'd seen once when we'd gone to Mexico.

"I am Estrella. You are Eliza?" She held up her floury hands and smiled.

I nodded. "I love your name," I said.

"It means 'star' in Spanish." She went back to kneading the dough. Above her head a string of red peppers hung on the wall. "When I was young, I planned to go to Hollywood and try out for the movies. I've always loved to sing."

"Did you ever go there?" I said.

Estrella shook her head. "I stayed in Mexico and had my babies." She winked at Paz.

"Now sometimes for Mexican weddings she sings in Rockport," Paz said.

"It's not quite the same as Hollywood," Estrella said, "but it earns money." She gave us each a lump of dough and showed us how to flatten it between our hands and clap. The sound echoed through the kitchen, like applause. We kept clapping until our tortillas were thin and floppy. Then Estrella laid the flat disks on the steaming griddle for a few seconds, turned them over, and sprinkled a handful of Mexican chocolate on top of each before cooking them a little longer.

"Now look!" Paz said. She reached into the refrigerator while Estrella rolled the tortillas into tubes. Paz stuck the

Reddi Wip can into the end of the tortilla and squirted it full of cream. "Texas tacos!" she said.

When I took my first bite, chocolate and cream dribbled onto Emily Dickinson. I ate two more.

Estrella asked me if my grandmother would like some tortillas.

"She only likes American food," I said.

"Paz is becoming like that, too. Perhaps, when the time comes, she will not want to return to Mexico."

Paz was holding the can of Reddi Wip upside down, squirting cream straight into her mouth.

I thanked them and headed back across the street. I couldn't wait for the next pier dance. I wondered if it was possible to fall in love with a whole family.

□

Mama Lacy was drinking a Lone Star and watching *The Red Shoes*. I'd seen it twice with Chloe. It was at the end where Victoria Page throws herself in front of a train. Then she lies there, dying, in her bloody toe shoes. It was the saddest scene I'd ever watched in a movie. I knew even a serial killer would break down if he saw it.

Mama Lacy said, "This picture just goes on and on and on."

"Why are you watching it?"

"What else is there to do?" she said. Her eyes stayed on the screen.

I remembered when she used to say there weren't enough hours in the day. Now she turned the TV on every morning and didn't even bother to switch channels.

Without taking her eyes off the screen, she said, "I ran across some old photos that might interest you, Elizabeth Jane. There in the album on the sofa. Take a look."

I knew exactly what I'd see. More pictures of Holly. "I don't have time. Aren't we going to see Daddy Jake?"

"You two go along without me," Mama Lacy said. "See if he'll put his book down for you."

I'd heard her tell Mom that his reading bird stories was a waste of time. I thought Mom would say how important stories were. Her whole life used to be stories. She wrote them and read them and daydreamed them. But she just smiled and kept quiet. Mom was a different person in Rockport.

Mama Lacy went back to watching her movie.

Mom was in the laundry room bleaching sheets. Mama Lacy told her to put Clorox in everything. I'd even seen her put a few drops in Porky's bathwater.

I told Mom about the dance. "I learned the salsa," I said.

She said I could go again on Friday as long as I didn't

tell Mama Lacy where I'd been. Then she said it might be better if I didn't mention that I was spending time across the street at the Castillos'. It was weird that Mom was forty years old and still couldn't tell the truth to her own mother.

I went upstairs and turned on the computer. Mail!

> *E-female*
> *Sears picked up the weights yesterday. Twenty-five more dollars to send them back. Big, strong guy. There was no choice since I strained my back. Mom exchanged the weights for a NordicTrack. As soon as I'm better, she wants me to do twenty minutes a day on this monster machine. I might refuse. There are limits. Summer shouldn't be like this.*
> *E-male*

> *E-male*
> *You're right. Summer shouldn't be like this. Mama Lacy still isn't trying to walk one single step. Maybe she's faking. She probably likes it better with us here, so she just pretends. I thought about hiding in the closet when I'm alone with her. I'll bet she makes sneak trips to the refrigerator for beer.*
> *E-female*

I hated the idea of Forrest lifting weights instead of reading. I knew his brain would get flabby.

□

Mom and I rode to Moonhaven along the bay road. She said she'd talked to Dad, who said Nacho had learned how to drag a full bag of garbage outside through the dog door.

"I miss Nacho so much," I said. "What if he forgets who I am? I've never been away from him so long."

Mom nodded. "Of course he might just appreciate you more by the end of summer. Who knows?"

I figured she was thinking of Dad. She didn't understand that with Nacho it was different. No long-distance talks.

We passed gray cottages with rickety skiffs in the driveways and front yards of sand, like Mama Lacy's.

"All the houses here look exactly alike."

She paused. "You miss Willow Street, don't you, darling?"

I didn't answer. I hated when she tried to guess what I was thinking. She'd learned about "active listening" from her psychiatrist, Dr. Barnwell. Sometimes it was better when she didn't listen at all.

"Wherever we decide to live," she said, "I just hope we *all* try a little harder with each other."

I knew she meant me. "Why don't I get to help decide where we live? It's my life, too."

"Indeed it is. When your father comes next weekend, we'll have a confab."

I was starting to hate that word. It rhymed with *flab* and *gab* and *slab* and *jab* and *blab*. Nothing good about words that sounded like that. "Why do you have to make such a big deal out of talking?"

Mom laughed. "You sound just like Mama. She says a doctor can't teach you how to talk any more than a plumber can teach you how to pee."

"I'm tired of hearing what she thinks."

"Oh, Liza. It just breaks my heart the way you and your father feel about Mama. She's aware of it, too. Believe me."

"It's her own fault. She doesn't care about anybody else."

Mom didn't answer at first. Then she said, "Liza, when you love someone, you try to keep on forgiving them. She *does* care."

Mom was getting on her pulpit. "Daddy Jake doesn't even love her anymore," I said.

Then she said, "They love each other in their own way. He has a hard time showing his feelings, and she's got some bitterness."

"Why?"

Mom sighed. "Being raised on a hog farm, she wanted to be more than a plumber's wife."

"She's a snob and a half," I said.

She didn't answer. We drove awhile. The air-conditioning kept dripping icy water on my feet. Dad never remembered to get the cars fixed.

Finally she said, "She's always felt insecure about herself, being self-educated and all. Remember how when she'd lose at Scrabble, she'd run get the dictionary and read it for an hour?"

I remembered how Holly and I used to laugh at the way Mama Lacy's lips moved when she read to herself. It was as if her voice were in there trying to escape.

"But why don't you stand up to her?" I said. We passed an amusement park with a water slide. A kid was up at the top, getting up his nerve to go down.

Mom glanced at me. "You sound very angry, Liza," she said.

"Stop telling me what I'm feeling!"

She sighed. We rode for a while. Then she said, "Mama is what she is, and I'm not going to fight with her."

"That's the trouble. *No one* fights for what they believe!"

"Mama Lacy does!" Mom smiled.

I hated talking in cars. You were trapped.

☐

Daddy Jake sat in his room reading. He didn't have a TV. He'd told them to take it away so he could read. On his bedside table he kept a photograph of Mama Lacy when she was younger. I remembered her yellow sun hat with the daisy in the front that she'd wear in her rose garden. I called it her Mary Poppins hat.

She didn't look like a blue-haired grandmother in a wheelchair then. When we went grocery shopping together, she'd always stop in produce to juggle. She could do three oranges at once and not drop one for almost two minutes. Every shopper would stop to look. Once she even came to my homeroom for show-and-tell.

When Daddy Jake saw us, he lowered his book to his lap but didn't close it. His eyebrows made a white hedge over his eyes.

"Número Uno didn't come?" He always called Mama Lacy that. Once he'd told me, "The main reason Número Uno married me was to get my pretty name. Would you rather be called Thelma Lacy or Thelma Bottomly?"

Mom sat on the edge of the bed. "Mama's got chores."

"Chores," he said. "At least I don't have those." I loved listening to him talk. He never used too many words, just said what he wanted and got it over with. Every word he chose was always the exact honest word for what he wanted to say.

I sat down on the floor beside his chair as the skinny nurse came into the room. "Mr. Lacy, did you take your insulin?" He nodded. I wanted to tell her to call him Jake.

I wondered if he felt like a different person at Moonhaven, without his birdhouses. Lately I didn't feel like a person at all. I felt invisible.

Now Daddy Jake was telling Mom about how the Moonhaven elevator had broken down. That meant he couldn't ride up the two floors to the dining room. He said, "The stairs were littered with old ladies."

Mom smiled. She always said he talked the way George Burns used to.

He looked at me. "I'm reading about a yellow-breasted chat," he said. He closed his book. "How's Rockport treating you? Guess you miss your friends. Especially the ballet dancer."

I shrugged. I couldn't talk to him with Mom around. Not about anything that mattered. He always asked me about Chloe. He had said someday she'd be "a heartbreaker." I sort of knew what he meant. You felt lucky whenever Chloe smiled at you. Her smile took up her whole face. I used to try to smile like her, walk like her, *be* her. Once when she dislocated her finger in fifth grade, she had to wear a splint; her perfect oval fingernail poked out the end of the bandage. I made a splint with a Popsicle stick for my own finger and wore it for three weeks until Chlo got hers off.

"Sometimes home is where the heart isn't." Daddy Jake smiled.

Mom's mouth went tight around the corners, like a contour sheet. I knew she wanted him to say I'd adjust soon.

"What's your favorite thing so far?" he said.

"A goat named Hector," I said.

"Hector, huh? Mine's pigeons," he said. "Learn plenty about home when you got pigeons."

I'd heard him say that before. He'd raced pigeons all his life. When I was little, we'd drive his pickup fifty miles to Beeville with the pigeons in cages in back. Then we'd release them. By the time we'd get back to Rockport, some of them would already be back home. A few got lost every year, but Daddy Jake always said they were the ones who knew Rockport wasn't their home, anyhow.

"How can you stand it here without your pigeons?" I said.

He didn't answer. He was looking at Mom. Then I saw she was upset. Her face was collapsing, like a limp pillow case. "I'll let you two visit a bit." She hurried out of the room.

I said, "What did I say wrong?"

He took my hand. "Nothing. Your mother's got your sister on her mind today. Can see it in her eyes."

"She keeps telling me to talk about my feelings, but she never talks about Holly."

He nodded. "One day she will. How you getting on with Número Uno?"

"Bad. She used to be fun once in a while. She doesn't even play games anymore. Or juggle."

He leaned forward in his chair. "She needs to be here with me where she can take it easy, get her meals."

"Why don't you convince her?"

"Ever try to force a canary to sing?" He smiled. "Liza, I'm going to confide in you. Today's a special day for me. Fifty years ago today I married my first wife."

"Marie?" I knew about Marie, but he seldom talked about her. I'd seen a picture of her once, standing in front of a white house with green shutters.

"I used to get up at six in the morning when I lived in Philadelphia," he said, "so I could watch out my window and see her ride by to work on the trolley."

"What did she do?"

He took off his glasses. "Wrote an advice column."

"What kind?"

"Lovelorn column for the *Saturday Evening Post*."

"A lovelorn column!"

"Yep. One day I sent her a dozen roses and asked her how you propose to a lovelorn columnist. She answered me right there in the column. Said she had no idea, but she'd sure like to know."

He explained how, after they were married, they lived in a town called Pumpkin Grove. She had a garden with some pumpkins, but mostly strawberries and raspberries. "The birds loved it. I was in heaven with Marie and all her berries," he said. "Then I went to war." His voice got softer. "The month before I got back from Germany, she wrote me that she'd met someone else." He took a breath. "After the divorce I moved to Rockport to raise pigeons and marry Número Uno." He stared out the window.

I waited. Outside, kids were laughing and yelling down below.

He reached for my hand. "Now for the secret. Don't tell. Rockport's never felt like home to me."

I tried turning his wedding ring around, but it wouldn't turn. "So why did you live your whole life here?"

He smiled. "It's home for Número Uno."

"Why did you let her move you to Moonhaven?" I said.

"She didn't move me anywhere. Moved myself."

"Why?" I said. I didn't believe him. It was her doing.

"Pork," he said. "Not tired of it yet?"

"Really, tell me."

"Just got tired of depending on her for everything. Here I've got all I need, except family. One day she'll admit she's lonely and join me."

Mom came back in. "Sorry," she said. "I just had to

get some air. The heat's too much today. Guess I need to go back to the house and lie down.''

Daddy Jake nodded. "Liza, know what you call a pig with no legs?''

I didn't.

"Ground pork,'' he said. "One of your grandmother's favorites.''

"We'll be back in a few days when I'm feeling better,'' Mom said.

"Isn't my confidante going to kiss me good-bye?'' he said.

I leaned down and kissed his cheek. I had a secret I wanted to tell him, too, but Mom was standing too close.

□

When we got home, Mama Lacy was watching *South Pacific,* her favorite movie. She knew all the words and sang along off-key. "Your friend called earlier,'' she said, not looking away from the movie. "Norris. Said he had some news.''

"You mean Forrest?''

She nodded and turned the volume up.

I stood between her and the TV, waving my arms around, trying to get her attention. The best thing of the entire week had just happened. And all Mama Lacy could do was sing "Happy Talk."

"What did he say?"

"He said to go turn on your computer."

I headed upstairs to check my E-mail. Sure enough.

E-female
I love my NordicTrack. I tried out for the track team and made it. I knew these feet were born for greatness.
E-male

Track? Forrest? I pictured his too-long feet, with the long second toes, speeding by his competitors. I tried not to be disappointed. At least he was happy. Still, I liked the old Forrest better. Soon he'd be hooking his thumbs in his belt loops, shouting, "Go, Cowboys!"

chapter 5

I'd gone to the pier dance twice. Beto never talked much, but that felt okay. Paz said he had other things on his mind. She didn't say what.

She offered to teach me how to Rollerblade. I told Mom, but she said she didn't want more broken bones to take care of.

"You used to love watching Holly roller-skate," I said.

Mom was cutting up carrots. "Rollerblades are different," she said.

I knew it was just an excuse. Lately she was afraid of everything. Last month it was stairs and steak. She kept telling me not to fall or choke.

Now she was upset because Dad had called at the last minute to say he wasn't coming down to Rockport. He had to fly to Dallas to pick up a shipment of teak elephants for his auction. It was typical.

All I could think about was Forrest, waiting. And Nacho,

wondering why I'd abandoned him. Maybe Dad didn't want to come down to Rockport. He always hated visiting Mama Lacy, but maybe he didn't even want me home for a visit. Every time I talked to him on the phone, he said he missed me. But maybe he was just saying that. Whenever I thought about it, I felt as if somebody had stuffed a wad of cotton in my throat.

"We've been buddies all year," he had said before I left Willow Street. But maybe he'd just been selling me on the idea of Rockport. Mama Lacy always said he was the world's best salesman. Yesterday when she'd heard Mom hang up on him, she said, "That man's so self-centered he forgets when the sun sets."

"Do you think he'll come *next* weekend?"

She didn't answer.

I touched her shoulder. I was sorry I'd brought up the subject of Dad. She seemed more upset than I was.

Pieces of carrot flew off the cutting board onto the floor, but she didn't even stop to pick them up. The thing about Mom is she always gets her hopes up that people will change. That's one thing I love about her. Sometimes it works because you hate more than anything to disappoint her.

□

When Paz asked me to go with them to Port Aransas to see the whooping cranes, I decided not to ask Mom.

Paz said her brother might drive their uncle's coffin truck.

"Coffin truck?"

She explained that their uncle lived in Rockport and made coffins. Beto helped him. Evenings and Saturdays Beto sometimes used the truck for his "secret business." Paz smiled and raised her eyebrows when she said that.

"What 'secret business'?" I said.

"One day I will tell you," she said.

I told her I'd love to go to Port Aransas. I knew that all I had to do was choose the time when Mom was day-dreaming, and she'd just say, "Uh-huh." I could tell her I was going to Tahiti and she'd say, "Uh-huh." The trouble was I forgot what a good listener Mama Lacy was.

Mom had picked up Daddy Jake from Moonhaven for dinner. She fixed Waldorf salad and pork chops and beets. Mom said I could help cook as long as I didn't mess up the kitchen. I figured Mama Lacy wouldn't like my special potatoes, because she was fussy about what she ate. She liked extra-well-done pork because "you have to be sure to kill all the bugs."

"What bugs?" I said.

"Telescopic. You can't see them."

"Microscopic!" I said.

The oven heated up the whole house. Thousands of dead bugs cooking.

Most of the dishes I made at home were ethnic. I loved

curries and pastas, but Mama Lacy said there was no food like good American food. I figured she'd always liked mummified meat and always would. She didn't eat my "pesty potatoes." I told her they were *pesto* potatoes, made with garlic, cheese, and basil.

"Can't taste the potato!" she said.

Daddy Jake was talking about his pigeon, número thirty-four, with iridescent green-tipped wings.

Mama Lacy said, "That bird was a lemon! Came home fast enough but then moseyed around on the roof all night."

I looked at Mom. She was daydreaming.

"Tomorrow I'm going to Port Aransas," I said, "to see whooping cranes."

Daddy Jake's eyebrows went up. "Quite a sight, those cranes. Probably won't see 'em in summer, though."

Mama Lacy looked at me. "Who are you going with?" She glanced at Mom, who was picking the raisins out of her Waldorf salad.

"The Castillos," I said. I figured she'd assume their mother was driving.

"Who's driving?" Mama Lacy said.

I hesitated. "Paz's big brother."

"That dark boy with the greasy hair," she said.

"His hair's beautiful. I think he just puts stuff on it to get it to stay back, that's all. It's long."

"I'll say it's long!" she said.

Mama Lacy asked Daddy Jake if he wanted some more leftover biscuits.

He didn't. "Those biscuits are old enough to vote," he said. "What's wrong with long hair? The Beatles had it."

Mom looked up from her raisin pile. "Go where?"

"Port Aransas. Just a few hours." I tried not to raise my voice.

Mama Lacy said, "The Spanish boy across the street. Likely doesn't have a license."

"He's not Spanish. He comes from Mexico," I said. "That means he's Mexican!"

"Watch your tone with your grandmother," Mom said.

"Have his license?" Mama Lacy said.

"Sure, he's old. At least eighteen," I said. I knew Beto was sixteen but figured no one else did.

"Eighteen!" Mama Lacy put her fork down. "That's plain too old."

"I'm not marrying him!"

Mom started clearing. "We'll talk about it later."

"It's dangerous going with a young driver," Mama Lacy said.

I pushed my chair back. "He just drives onto the ferry and sits there till it reaches the other side."

Daddy Jake laughed. "Golly Moses. What a fuss over cranes!"

"Liza," Mom said, "enough."

"It's not like I'm going alone with Beto. I'm practically baby-sitting. His sister's going, and she's about two feet tall!" Now I was making fun of Paz. I almost sounded like Mama Lacy. "She can't help being short," I added.

"I'll say only one thing," Mama Lacy said. "People like that don't have any education, and folks judge you here by the company you keep. They're wetbacks!"

"Thelma, stop that now!" Daddy Jake pounded the table with his fist.

"Mama!" Mom raised her voice for once. "They're called illegals, and I don't want to hear any more about this subject."

I looked straight at Mom. "You didn't mind that Tina was illegal when she cleaned our house every week!" Somehow I'd swallowed Mama Lacy's voice. "What's wrong with the Castillos? They have fun. They own a pet goat named Hector."

Daddy Jake said, "What's Número Uno say to that?"

"Goats belong on farms!" Mama Lacy said. "Folks keep to their own here, and you need to know the way things are if you're making your home here."

I looked at Mom, but she'd closed her eyes.

"My home's on Willow Street in San Antonio," I said.

60

No one answered.

Daddy Jake said, "You know what they call a boomerang that doesn't come back? A stick."

I didn't smile. "You could at least stand up for me."

"Let her go see the cranes," Daddy Jake said. Then he turned to Mama Lacy. "If folks judge you by the company you keep, maybe you better stop hanging around with me."

Mom banged the dishes as she put them in the dishwasher.

"That boy's truck comes and goes all hours of the night," Mama Lacy said. "I'll tell you right now that he's involved in some funny business."

"What do you mean, 'funny business'?" I said. I remembered Paz saying "secret business."

She paused. "Could be any number of things, I suppose."

"Enough!" Mom said. "I can't take this. When Chloe arrives, I'll take you two to Port Aransas to see the cranes. End of discussion."

"All right," I said. "But it won't be the same." My hands were fists. Why couldn't Mom understand that it wasn't just cranes?

☐

The pork smell had crept upstairs to spend the night.

I went upstairs so I could talk to Forrest.

E-male
My grandmother gets away with saying horrible things
about people because no one stands up to her (she
even hates my pesto potatoes). Mom thinks keeping
peace is more important than what's right. I'll never
be like that. It's not genetic, I hope. Congratulations on
making the track team.
E-female

I got up and stood at the window, gazing toward the lighthouse. If only Nacho were beside me. And Chloe. I wanted to tell her everything. She listened better than anyone I ever knew. With her whole body instead of just her ears.

In a way it was almost a sacrifice to have such a perfect best friend. Still, I loved her too much for it to feel like a sacrifice. Guys looked at her more than they did me. She thought they didn't like her because of her disability, but she was wrong. When she was lip-reading, she listened so hard with her eyes that everyone grew to love her. She put lemon on her hair and sat out every day so she had blond streaks and a great tan by the end of May. She moved in a wavy way, with her feet turned out, like a dancer.

I couldn't wait to see her. Still, I was worried. Sometimes when we'd talked on the phone during the last year, she'd seemed different. We hadn't laughed as much as usual, and a couple of times there were big spaces when neither of us said anything at all. Mom said friends could grow apart in a year, but I told her that would never happen to us. In my head I kept repeating, "Heart/heart."

I heard the phone ring downstairs. Dad called Mom so much. I made up excuses so I wouldn't have to talk to him for a while, but Mom seemed to have forgiven him.

It wasn't fair that I couldn't talk every day to my friends. When I complained, Mom said, "It was generous of Mama to put in that phone jack upstairs so you can E-mail. Now the least you can do is to respect her wishes."

"Except Chloe doesn't have E-mail. It's not fair," I'd said.

"She'll be here soon," she said. Then she put on her patient look and said the most obvious thing: "The world's not always a fair place, Liza."

□

Mama Lacy was sitting in front of the TV when I went down. "Your friend called."

"Forrest?"

"No, the one from Houston. Cleo."

"Chloe! Just now? She must have known I was thinking about her. What did she say? Why didn't you call me?" Inside my head I was saying, She's coming. She's coming.

"Said to call her back. I thought you were asleep already.

But make it snappy and feed Porky first. He's hungry.''
Mama Lacy wheeled into her room.

I could hardly keep still until I fed Porky. I opened the
refrigerator to get the cat food and saw a jar of pickles.
Ever since she was little, Chloe always loved to drink pickle
juice straight out of the jar. I picked up the jar and took a
tiny, sour sip. I wanted to like it but still didn't.

I headed for the phone. Chlo answered on the first ring
and told me she'd just gotten back from practicing ballet
four hours in a row.

"I can't wait to see you," I said.

"No, my mom's late picking me up," she said.

I knew she hadn't heard me. I could tell whenever her
answers didn't match my questions. She hated asking anyone, even me, to repeat when she didn't hear.

"When do you get here?" I said.

She said her bus arrived next Friday at three. Only five
days! When I started telling her about the Castillos, Mama
Lacy yelled, "You've talked long enough!"

"I can hear every word she says," Chloe said, "even
though I'm in Houston and practically deaf! I think you've
got some right to make noise yourself now and then."

I agreed. Chloe always talked about rights. Student, disa-
bled, female, animal. Ever since she was little, she'd orga-
nized protests for what she believed in.

"Hang up now, Liza," Mama Lacy said. "You're running up my bill."

"I guess I need to go, Chlo," I said.

We said good-bye. I knew she wouldn't agree to call me back because she hated talking on phones.

Then I just stood there, thinking how I had lost all my rights. Why couldn't I make noise once in a while? I lived here, too. I went upstairs and opened my trombone case. I hadn't played even once since we'd arrived. I took out the mute that Chloe had given me for my birthday. Then I ran downstairs with my trombone. I stopped halfway between Mom's door and Mama Lacy's and started playing "When the Saints Go Marching In." I marched up the hall the way Golobick had taught us in band. I picked up my knees and held my head high.

Mom's door flew open, and she stuck her head out. "Liza? What on earth? Have some respect for Mama Lacy, for goodness' sake!"

"I'm sick of having respect, and I'm sick of being quiet!" I felt like throwing my horn on the floor, but I knew how much it cost. I'd never get another one.

Mom said, "This isn't easy for me either, believe m-me!" Her voice was shaking. I hadn't heard her stutter in a while.

I almost said I was sorry. How could I promise myself

one day to be nicer to her, then completely forget? I said, "Don't I have some rights in this house?"

She paused, then lowered her voice to a whisper. "Liza, why don't you go down to the beach and play your trombone? You can blast away down there, and no one will mind."

I unscrewed the mouthpiece from my horn and wiped it on my T-shirt. "Why don't you go write your stories on a desert island, and then no one will ever have to read them!"

Mom just stood there trying not to cry. She looked exhausted. I used to be so proud of her, especially after she'd published her novel. Now she seemed like everyone else's mother.

I wanted more than anything to say I was sorry, but the words clogged up in my throat. I wasn't sure exactly what I was sorry about. I was sorry I was a mean person, and I was sorry that I didn't love my grandmother, and I was sorry I didn't have a family like the Castillos, and I was sorry that Dad didn't care enough to come get me. Most of all, I was sorry that Holly had died!

But I wanted to tell Mom that none of it was her fault. Still, whose fault was it?

I knew Chlo would be proud of me for asserting my rights, but I wasn't proud. Sometimes I felt as if my heart had a thick orange rind around it. I turned and ran upstairs before Mom could see I was crying.

chapter 6

"We need to shop for Chloe," Mom said. "I know she has a strict diet."

She's coming. She's coming. She's coming. It's all I could think about.

At Safeway we bought carob, instead of chocolate, to make Chloe's brownies. I figured we'd eat them fast before the humidity turned them into Rockport mush.

As we walked through produce, I picked up three limes and tried to juggle the way Mama Lacy used to. Mom said, "Of course, she'll comment on Mama's girth as soon as she arrives." Mom put her hands on her hips and rolled her eyes. "Liza, how can your grandmother eat all that pig!"

"Chloe's bringing her toe shoes," I said. "I can't believe I know an almost professional ballerina." I was squeezing every single avocado. Finally I found the best one. My fingers made dents in it. It was huge. Almost ripe enough for guacamole. I knew Chloe loved it with carrot sticks. I bought Fritos for me.

Mom nodded. "I'm proud of her, too. It's not easy to stick to your dream."

Stick to her dream. That was Chlo. She was the only person I ever knew who stuck to what she believed in, no matter what.

Mom said I could do more cooking while Chlo visited. She said she'd appreciate the break. "I'm getting so tired of that little tiny kitchen. If Mama Lacy would only agree to go to Moonhaven with Daddy. It's clear she shouldn't stay alone anymore, but you know how she is."

I knew exactly. I'd heard Mama Lacy say she'd live and die on Raht Street. Dad said she'd bought a fifty-year termite protection plan on her house. I figured she'd be one hundred and twenty-two when it ran out.

I said, "Can't you just tell her she has to go there? *We* have a life, too." I picked up the limes, which had rolled under the potato bin.

"It's hard to make people do things they don't want to do."

"Really? I hadn't noticed."

Mom was already headed for the tomatoes. I was glad she hadn't heard me because I was too excited about Chloe to have another fight. I bought squash and broccoli and lentils and tofu. One night I knew I'd make pasta puttanesca: capers and tomatoes and olives and garlic and basil. Any leftovers you could find.

☐

As Mom and I were putting the groceries away, Mama Lacy yelled from her room, "I suppose you only bought health food!"

Mom put her hands over her ears and smiled at me.

Then Mama Lacy yelled, "Elizabeth Jane, make me a Miracle Whip and tomato sandwich. You make them better than your mother. Wash your hands first!"

I smothered the white bread in Miracle Whip the way she liked it and put the sandwich on the counter. Then I made carob brownies and put them in the oven. I knew we had to leave to get Chlo, so I asked Mama Lacy to take out my brownies when they were done.

☐

Chloe's bus was late, so Mom and I got drinks out of the machine. She drank iced tea, but I couldn't finish my Coke because my stomach was flipping around.

I'd washed my hair and forked it out with a kitchen fork to make it as straight as I could. When I looked in the mirror at the bus station, it was already frizz. Summer in Rockport made my hair into the worst Tuffy pad. I knew when Chloe climbed down from the bus, the first thing I'd see would be her sun-streaked hair. It was so shiny and smooth that she always had to toss it back off her face. Her hair always knew what move her body was going to make before Chloe knew.

I told Mom I might trade my ears for Chloe's hair.

''Darling, that would be a bad trade. Your good hearing is something to be grateful for. Chloe has a hard time in the world.''

I wondered what it would be like to look like Chloe. People always turned to stare at her, even though she never noticed. Her green eyes squinted a little, and I always knew she was seeing straight inside my brain. Her mouth was a pink candy heart that said, ''Kiss me.'' Maybe you wouldn't need to hear every single thing if you looked like that.

Mom saw the bus before I did, and I ran outside and looked in every window. Then people started getting off. Mom and I kept watching for Chlo. ''Maybe she's not coming,'' I said. We waited some more.

Finally Mom put her hand on my shoulder and said, ''There she is, darling!'' Chlo stood on the top step of the bus. Her hair was braided, then twisted around and around on top of her head.

''Chlo!'' I jumped up the steps to hug her. The bus driver asked if we'd mind finishing our hug off the bus.

She kissed me on both cheeks in that French way, like her mom used to. Then she said, "You got an Afro!"

I told her it was just humidity. "You had your ears pierced!" I said.

She touched her right one. "I got these pearl studs from Daddy for my birthday. I wear them all the time now, day and night, wet or dry."

"They're beautiful. *You're* beautiful!" I said.

She wore a long green shirt, belted over a flowered skirt with sandals. Usually she wore shorts and tennies like me. Her green suitcase was round like a hatbox and had a picture of pink toe shoes on the side.

"You've got more freckles," she said. "You look cute, like your dad."

"I hate them, but you know how I get in summer."

While we walked to the car, Chloe was talking about how much she liked Houston. Her voice made my feet go faster.

Mom asked how she liked her new house.

"I spend most of my time at the studio practicing."

"Is your new room emerald green?" I said. The chrome burned my fingers as I opened the car door.

Mom put the luggage on the front seat so Chloe and I could sit in back together where she could hear better.

"My wallpaper has gigantic morning glories," she said, "but I don't care. I'm gone so much." Chloe talked about her dance teacher. "Ms. Cuddeback's tall for a ballerina. She danced with the Royal and taught me to do twenty fouettés in a row."

Mom had to hold the steering wheel with tissues to keep from burning her hands. She was asking about Chlo's parents, talking extra-loud. Chloe said her father had season tickets for the Astros, and her mother had an art exhibition coming up. Even though Chloe's parents were getting divorced, she saw them both all the time.

"I can't believe I'm finally here," she said. "I haven't done a single thing but diet and dance, and I can't wait to just hang with you, Liza. Watch TV and veg."

I hadn't watched much TV in Rockport so far. Mama Lacy turned it off after *Wheel of Fortune* and said she needed her beauty rest. I hadn't even gone to the pier dance last Friday because Mom felt lonely and wanted company.

Most nights I just read, but I knew Chloe wouldn't want to do that. Chloe only liked videotapes and said anything worth saying was worth saying out loud. I guess she had more respect for ears than the average person.

When we pulled up in front of Mama Lacy's, I waved at Paz, who was Rollerblading on the sidewalk.

"Who's that?" Chloe said. She swung her ballet box at her side.

"Paz. She's really fun."

"Do you baby-sit her?"

"No. She doesn't look it, but she's twelve and already knows what she wants to do with her life. She's getting growth hormones because she quit growing. I hope it works. She has an older brother." I wanted to tell Chlo about Beto, but not until we were alone.

We went inside. She looked around. "It's small," she said. "The way your grandmother used to talk about this house, I thought it would be humongous."

"My room's the best," I said. "C'mon up."

We carried her stuff up to my roof room, where Chloe put her things on the cot. "It's great," she said. "It suits you." Then she looked out the dormer window toward Candy Land. "That's kind of cute. Like a playhouse or something."

"It's not boring, like most houses."

She agreed and looked through the other dormer window toward the lighthouse. "That's cool!" she said.

"I really love it. It blinks every eight seconds."

She smiled. "Did you ever go up in it?"

"I doubt you can," I said. "Maybe people live in it."

"How do you know? We should find out."

I agreed. Chloe always dreamed stuff, then made her dreams come true. I'd made a pact with myself a thousand times to try to be like her.

We both wanted a snack before bed. I remembered the brownies, but Chloe took only one bite. "It's like eating a Lego," she said. Mama Lacy had left them in the oven too long.

Chloe ate carrot sticks and pickles. I had Chunky Monkey ice cream with double fudge chocolate syrup. Then we switched on *Letterman*. We were laughing really loud when Mama Lacy's voice boomed from the bedroom, "Girls!"

"Oh, Jesus!" Chloe whispered. "The volleyball voice."

Mama Lacy called out, "What's that I hear?"

"David Letterman!" I tried to yell even louder than she did. Chloe laughed. Her laugh always rippled up and down like a piano.

"Well, whoever it is, it's too late," Mama Lacy yelled.

Then Mom came out of her room. "Turn it down a bit, girls. Mama can't sleep."

"Chloe can't hear it when it's low. You know that, Mom. Let's go upstairs and talk," I said.

"You're a good sport," Mom said.

Chloe wrinkled her nose. She hated good sports.

Upstairs she looked through the neat stacks of clothes in her suitcase and took out her leotard. "I need to practice while I'm here," she said. "Ms. Cuddeback says a day without practice is like a cream puff without cream." She laid her toe shoes on the cot next to her favorite stuffed lion, Belvedere.

I got in bed and told Chloe about Hector's diet.

She just stared out the window. "It's awfully early," she said. "In summer I stay up till two A.M."

"Fridays there's always a dance at the pier," I said.

"What sort of dance?"

"Salsas, waltzes, everything. You'll be the star."

"Waltzes? I went to a Dead concert last week," she said. "You wouldn't believe the people." She talked about a skinny guy in a skeleton costume.

Then I told Chloe about Beto. "He even plays the guitar. He's part of a mariachi band."

"How do you know? Maybe he's just scoping you out to see what impresses you."

"He isn't like that." I'd already decided not to tell her about the Castillos being illegal. She wasn't prejudiced at all, but she hated anyone who wasn't completely honest. "He drives a pickup and helps build coffins. He's a serious person."

"Is he tall?"

"Gigantic," I said. "*I* even feel small beside him."

"Great, Liza!" she said. "We won't have to carve your shoes!"

We started laughing and remembering. In seventh grade I'd been invited to a dance by the shortest guy in our class; I was the tallest girl. I didn't want to go, but Mom kept saying I should. "Once you get there, you'll forget about being tall," she said. Then she'd surprised me with an expensive pair of *one-inch* satin heels! I'd gone straight to Chloe's to show her the disaster shoes. I stood there, five feet nine, a hulking monster. Still, I couldn't hurt Mom's feelings. Then Chloe got a plan.

She sneaked her father's hunting knives into her room; we each took one shoe and began carving. Finally the one-inch heels were gone, leaving two ragged, bumpy, uneven satin flats. At the dance she'd watched me rock back and forth all evening like a drunk.

Now we couldn't stop laughing. I knew her laugh was echoing all the way downstairs.

"I've missed you so much, Liza," Chloe said. "There's not one single person in all of Houston like you."

"You haven't met every single one of them yet," I said.

"I don't need to," she said.

Neither of us talked for a while. Finally I got up and went over to her bed. Her eyes were closed. Her thick lashes looked like tiny fans that a flamenco dancer would flutter.

"Chlo?" I said. I wanted to tell her how glad I was that she was finally here beside me again.

She didn't answer. Maybe she was asleep.

I held up my palm. "Heart/heart," I whispered.

chapter 7

E-female
I strained my Achilles tendon. The coach says my feet
are "too long for track." I was a jock for only three days.
E-male

E-male
I'm really sorry about your tendon. It must have been
your weak point. I know you would have liked being a
jock, but remember you said once, "Who would come
to a foot doctor with wrecked feet?"
E-female

I turned off the computer when I heard Chloe coming back upstairs after breakfast. I hadn't told her that Forrest and I had been E-mailing. I wasn't sure why I kept it a secret. But you had to understand Forrest to appreciate him. Besides, my feelings for him were sealed away, like my birthstone ring that I kept in its velvet box.

□

Chlo wore her new Avia tennies: purple, pink, and black stripes. On Willow Street she had always gone barefoot and hated designer shoes. I missed her dusty toes. I wore my blue Keds. We headed for the beach.

We stepped over tar blotches that looked like blobs of melted licorice.

"Look at the dead jellyfish. Gross. Are you and Forrest still an item?" she said.

She'd read my mind. She could always do that. I shrugged. "Hard to tell, long distance."

"You know what? You can do better." She kicked some rocks out of her path.

"What do you mean?" I knew she thought Forrest was a weird science type. She was right, but that was another thing I loved about him.

"He's all thought, no action," she said. "My mom says that same thing about artists who just talk about being artists."

"He ran track this summer." I left out for how long.

Chloe stopped and took off her shoes, swinging them as she walked. I kept mine on because I still had blisters from the last time I went barefoot. I remembered the time on Willow Street when Chloe and I had tried baking peanut-butter cookies on the sizzling sidewalk and ended out hosing away the whole mess.

We stopped for Slushees at Taco Cabana. Chloe got blueberry, and I got peach. I was sure Ms. Gonzalez made them extra big because she knew I was Paz's friend.

We walked along backward, sucking on ice. We used to walk backward all the way home from the school bus. Now we watched a few kids playing in the sand, but mostly we had the beach to ourselves. Chlo was with me again; nothing else mattered.

I told her about the girl next door. "I haven't met her yet, but I've seen her from a distance. She looks like Uma Thurman. She's a Senior Scout and even *friends* with Mama Lacy."

"I thought the most you had to do was help an old person across the street," Chloe said. "The water's like a great warm bathtub. Let's go in."

We took off our shorts. Chloe had on a new bikini with pink unicorns all over it. I wore my faded blue one-piece. Forrest called it shy blue.

The mud on the bottom oozed between my toes like oatmeal. The water stayed shallow forever here. I imagined Chloe and me wading to Cuba. We'd live on avocados until Beto arrived in a kayak and played his guitar in the moonlight.

We walked a long way in the shallows. Then Chloe dived under. Her hair streamed to the top. I jumped under. Then we floated on our backs awhile, not talking. We'd spent a hundred summers like this, floating side by side.

We treaded water while we talked. Chloe said she hadn't had time to make friends yet in Houston because she was always practicing. "There are so many ditzes out there, Liza. You wouldn't believe it!"

"It must be lonely, though. What about guys?"

"Well, there's this one creep. You know those types that always like me? Like scrubbed faces, not one whisker yet? Ironed shirts and creased pants? When all I want is Sean Penn."

"Chloe, every type likes you. Even Forrest thinks you're cute."

"He does? I thought he only liked bookish types."

"What do you mean? I'm not a bookish type."

"No, but you have a tendency, Liza. You could be a bookish type if you're not careful." She splashed me.

I wanted to stay in the water forever, listening to her voice and the ripple laugh. I could feel the sun baking my face. I knew Mama Lacy would point out my sunburn later, and freckles, but I didn't even care. The greatest thing in the whole world was hanging out with your best friend.

I talked to Chloe about the lighthouse. "Don't you think

it's weird that only boats get a tower all their own so they won't forget where home is?''

"Let's go see it!'' she said. We raced each other back to our towels.

The fog was starting to move in as we walked up the beach together toward the lighthouse, which was about a mile away. Chlo kept getting ahead of me. Then I'd hurry to catch up. She was talking about her recital when she'd danced Juliet.

I heard a foghorn. Then we were standing at the base of the lighthouse. It was smaller than I remembered, gray and weathered, not white and glowing the way it looked from far away.

The rusty spiral stairway twisted around and around the inside like a huge bedspring. Chloe started climbing really fast ahead of me. I'd been following her somewhere all my life. I'd never minded too much.

I was out of breath when I reached the top. My head felt light, as if it could float my whole body up into the air. I loved the mildewy smell, like our cellar on Willow Street.

Chloe put her face up to the cloudy window on the locked door at the top of the stairs. She rubbed the crusty stuff with her fingers to clear off a peephole. No one was inside, just a panel, like the dashboard of a car. The light blinked on and off, eight seconds between flashes. Forrest would say it was scientifically programmed, but to me it seemed like magic. It was great that somehow the lighthouse knew on its own what to do.

Chloe said, "This lighthouse is boring! We're missing *The Young and the Restless*. Let's go." She said she'd already been to three rock concerts, four ballets, and two baseball games in Houston. In San Antonio her father had always called her the fun magnet.

☐

We got back just in time so Chloe could watch her soap. A bubbly blond named Kimberly had broken up with a bumbling jock named Joshua. Kimberly put her curly head down on the polished kitchen table and sobbed hysterically.

Chloe said, "Oh, no, Jesus Christ, not again, Josh!"

I wondered if Mama Lacy could hear her. Once Mom had told me that when she'd used the Lord's name in vain as a little girl, Mama Lacy had made her drink picante sauce.

Then I looked out front and saw Beto's truck pulling into our driveway.

"He's never been over here before in his life," I said.

Mama Lacy's voice boomed out, "Is that boy here? About time!" She wheeled herself into the kitchen.

"What do you mean?" I said.

"I decided to put a patio in the backyard. I heard the Castillo boy knew something about laying bricks, so I hired him."

"I thought you didn't want him over here!"

"Can't hurt anything," she said. "He's working outside. Go see if Porky's back there. I can't find him." She had her hand to her chest and was taking quick breaths. That meant palpitations.

"Why doesn't she want him over here?" Chloe said as we went out.

I shrugged. "His hair's too long, or he's too tall, or something!" I felt guilty about leaving out the fact that he was illegal, but I knew she'd just get all upset. Chloe was *such* a fanatic about telling the truth.

I'd almost forgotten why. We never talked about it. When she was eight years old, she'd shown up at my front door on Willow Street late at night, her face all pale and scared. "My parents lied to me all these years," she said. "My very own parents lied to me!" Somehow she'd found out by accident that she was adopted.

"But it was a good lie," I had said, "so you wouldn't feel bad. They love you exactly the same as my parents love me."

Even though it was summer, she had just stood there at the door, frozen-looking. "There's no such thing as a *good* lie," she'd said. "Don't ever say that to me again. And don't ever lie to me, Liza, or we won't be friends anymore."

We'd never, ever talked again about her being adopted.

☐

We watched Beto lay bricks. His portable radio was playing. That meant Chlo wouldn't be able to hear the conversation.

I kept looking at her feet while she talked. Since second grade I'd wanted those perfect toes. They'd always been smooth and even as piano keys, but now they had bumps and blisters from her toe shoes.

"Do you miss Mexico?" she said as she picked up Porky and began petting him.

Beto nodded. "One day I will go back."

She glanced at me. She hadn't heard.

"He's going back someday."

Chloe said Houston felt as much like home to her now as San Antonio used to. She said ballet was her life. As long as she could dance, she didn't care where she lived. She didn't mention missing me or Willow Street. She didn't even tell him about not having made a single friend in Houston yet. She had a tendency to keep bad stuff to herself. I wondered if she really was happy since she'd moved.

Home was still my main thing. I thought a lot about Willow Street. I missed my place on the roof. Chloe and I had been up there together on the night of the blue moon. That was when she'd told me that she was leaving San Antonio forever.

Beto showed Chloe how to smooth off the mortar with a stick. He said he'd finish only part of it today, so he'd be back soon. It was weird how before I wasn't supposed to see him, yet here he was in Mama Lacy's own backyard. I saw her peeking through the curtain.

I remembered the time when I was eight years old and Mama Lacy was visiting in San Antonio. She was making potato soup when she cut off the tip of her finger in the food processor. Mom had rushed her to the emergency room, and I'd stayed home with Holly. When I'd dumped the mess of potatoes and blood into the sink, I'd discovered the tip of Mama Lacy's finger. I carried it in the palm of my hand to the front yard and planted it under the sycamore. I never told anyone, not even Holly. I'd pretended a bush would grow in our yard and bloom with fingertips. Then I'd pick the best one and give it back to Mama Lacy.

We'd been watching Beto lay bricks for a long time when Paz arrived from across the street with a plate of big pastries that she called *buñuelos*. They looked like Frisbees sprinkled with cinnamon and sugar. Paz said she liked to spread hers thick with peanut butter and jelly.

"Por favor? I can hold him?" She held her hands out

to Chloe, who handed Porky to her. "His fur is matted," Paz said. "Tell your grandmother that Porky is needing beer." Paz explained her theory of animal nutrition to Chloe. I noticed she kept using Spanish words mixed in with her English. She seemed nervous. For some reason Chloe made people feel that way.

I was watching Beto spread mortar onto the bricks and place them in straight rows. I loved how the yard used to be just dry grass and gopher holes. Now it was almost a patio. Chloe and I had always loved things that used to be something else, like butterflies or mummies.

I thought how Mama Lacy's patio might be there for a hundred years. Maybe forever.

We sat at the picnic table under the mesquite tree and drank lemonade with our *buñuelos*. Chloe said they were the best thing she'd ever eaten. Paz said lemonade made Hector bashful. Chloe did most of the talking, all about Houston and ballet. Beto kept looking at her. But then he wiped his face with the back of his hand, and I thought I saw him wink at me. But maybe he just had mortar in his eye.

Then I saw the star tattoo on his ring finger. I couldn't stop looking.

"It's his *estrella*," Paz said, "in honor of my mother."

"It's beautiful, just like she is," I said.

Chloe just stared at it. Maybe she hadn't heard us.

Paz handed me the plate and said, "Give the *buñuelos* to your grandmother. Tell her about the *cerveza* for Porky. And do not forget my birthday party," she said.

When Beto and Paz left, Chloe and I went back inside and sat on the sofa. Chloe pulled the old blanket off the sofa and sat down. She took off her sandals and applied a coat of What's Up Pink? over the old Kiss Me Coral.

"What do you think of Beto?" I said.

"He's way cool."

"I knew you'd think so. He looked at you a lot."

She shook her head. "He probably just couldn't believe how much I talk. You know how I do. It's like my voice has a forever battery. Like the Energizer, I keep on going!" She stood up and made chugging sounds. "I hate myself so much when I run off at the mouth, but I've tried, and I just can't stop." She sank down again in her chair, put her head back, and looked at the sky. She was biting her lip.

"Why? Beto was listening to every word you said. He even noticed your great toes. I could tell." Chloe never understood how amazing she was. Maybe being hard-of-hearing was like wearing blinders.

"Not even!" she said. She put the cap back on the polish and blew on her toes. "I've decided it doesn't matter to me what guys think, anyway. All I'm ever going to do my whole life is dance. Guys take up way too much time."

"What about Beverly Hills? What about the swimming pool and the personal trainer and Justin and Graham?" She'd named her kids a long time ago.

She shook her head. "Changed my mind. Since we moved last year, I've decided not to get attached. Ever again. Period. It's easier, in case you have to leave again."

She was looking away, blinking her eyes. For the first time I wondered if Chloe had really been too busy to write me very often since she moved. I'd written her a ton of letters she never answered. Maybe she was working on getting less attached to me. Getting on with her life. My fingers felt cold. I wanted to reach out and touch her shoulder, but she never liked people to feel sorry for her.

"I can tell exactly what you're thinking, Liza," she said, "every time you look at Beto. It's so obvious! You get too attached to people."

I just looked at her. She had no idea what I'd been thinking. "Me? I'm not the one who's attached," I said, even though I knew I was.

She reached for her Rave nail polish and polished just her pinkies. "I don't want to talk about Beto anymore. Okay? It's a waste of time. He'll just leave and go back to Mexico, anyway." She stood up and started doing her stretches, her back turned to me.

She wasn't the only one who knew about tendencies. I

knew that guys scared her, and I knew that no matter what she said, she wanted a long-term boyfriend more than anything else. I wanted to tell her to be honest about her own feelings, but I knew any talk about honesty would just start a fight. Then I'd have to be the one to make up. Like always.

I remembered the most stupid fight we ever had. We were in sixth grade and eating oatmeal at my house. She always put raisins in hers. I put butter and brown sugar on mine. She had just told me that her mother was reading this book called *You Are What You Eat*.

"Your brain is pure sugar, Liza," she said.

"Yours is the size of a raisin," I said.

We started laughing and smearing oatmeal all over each other's faces. Then I ran and got Dad to take our picture. She hated that idea! She yelled that I had no right to tell him to take her picture when she looked so dumb. I was scared that we'd never make up. Finally I promised her I'd throw away the picture and not show it to anyone. I even wrote a note and put it in her desk at school. "I miss you and I'm sorry. Heart/heart."

I was never sure why *I* was always the one to be sorry.

"Do you want to go upstairs and practice?" I said. "I want to see you dance."

"God, I thought you'd never ask!" she said. We headed up together.

c h a p t e r 8

E-female
I might have to go to the Grand Canyon next week with
my parents. When are you coming back?
          E-male
P.S. I hate canyons.

E-male
My dad still hasn't shown up. Maybe he likes it better
home alone. At least Chloe's here.
          E-female
P.S. Be careful.

Estrella wanted to do all of our hair for Paz's birthday party.
Paz said that my hair was just the kind her mother loved to
work on.

"What kind is that?" I asked.

"She says you have smart hair. It is always knowing
what it wants."

While Paz was getting her perm, I looked out the window

and saw Hector, pacing back and forth. Paz said Hector had been bored all day because she'd made the mistake of feeding him dill pickles for his runny nose. She said she'd forgotten that "pickles cause goat boredom."

Chloe decided on a "Mexican French braid." "*Muy complicado,*" Paz said. Very complicated. While Estrella braided, she sang a love song in Spanish. Paz sat on a high stool, looking at her mother. I imagined Estrella singing on a stage at the Hollywood Bowl.

Chloe looked great when she was done, but she always looked great.

I was getting sleepy, waiting for my haircut. The heat made me sleepy. The Castillos didn't have air-conditioning, just ceiling fans that blew your hair up in the air. If you had the kind of hair that moved.

"My hair's always been too curly," I said. "Don't ever cut yours off, Chlo." I knew if I had hair like hers, I'd never cut it in my entire life.

"Where's Beto?" Chloe asked Paz.

Paz shrugged. She was always mysterious about him.

"*Listo,* Eliza?" Paz said. "Ready?" I climbed up in the chair and warned Estrella how my hair shrank to half its size from wet to dry. I reminded her of how my ears stuck out and my neck went on and on.

"You worry about your looks too much, Liza," Chloe said.

I laughed. "That's easy for you to say!" I could see chunks of my red hair dropping to the floor. I closed my eyes. Estrella was taking off so much, but I hated to hurt her feelings. I remembered how once when I got home from the beauty shop, Holly swore my hair looked like red AstroTurf.

Estrella turned my chair around and began cutting the sides. Paz was laughing. I didn't open my eyes because I was afraid I was starting to look like Hector.

Then Estrella started with the blow dryer. I couldn't believe she'd use one on me because every time I tried, my hair frizzed. But things were already beyond hope, so what did it matter as long as it made her happy? She pulled my hair away from my head with the hairbrush until it hurt, then held the hot dryer so close to my head it burned. I hoped Forrest turned out to be right about suffering building character.

I could feel the brush going out, under, under, out, under, under. Then it didn't hurt anymore. Estrella's hands felt like feathers touching my head. The ceiling fan made a whirring sound that I could barely hear above the noise of the dryer and Estrella's voice singing another love song. I felt warm and sleepy and wanted to stay in that chair in their kitchen forever.

Then Estrella said, "Eliza." That was all she said, but the way she said it was like "I love you."

I opened my eyes, then blinked and looked again. I looked wonderful! My hair formed a smooth red mushroom that framed my face. Just the tops of my ears were covered, and my bangs were turned under and stopped just above my eyebrows. My eyes looked huge.

Paz cheered.

"You look like a Paris model!" Chloe said. She was right. I did. I wished Forrest were there to see me.

Then Estrella showed me how to use the dryer and styling gel. "Every morning you must pull out and under, always blowing with the dryer," she said.

Even though I loved the way I looked, I knew I wouldn't end out doing it every morning. I didn't have that much character. But I would do it for special occasions.

We thanked Estrella and then helped string the pink birthday lights over the Candy Land porch. It was just getting dark, but they already shone like colored stars.

I'd worn my khaki shorts and my old Achy Breaky Heart T-shirt that Holly had given me. I always saved it for special occasions. Chloe wore her pink halter top and white shorts with black sequins that spelled out "Houston Rockets" on the back pockets. She never used to wear flashy things.

The table had a pink crepe paper tablecloth and a burro piñata hanging from a hook on the ceiling. Paz said, "I have a surprise. I have learned the Pledge of Allegiance by memory." She recited it and made only one mistake near the end.

I said, "That's almost perfect, but instead of *invisible,* it's *indivisible. Forrest likes the word *indivisibility* because it's the only word with six *i*'s in it."

"He is smart," Paz said.

"And weird," Chloe whispered.

Paz introduced us to her twin cousins, Luna and Luz. They were about eight and wore dresses I'd seen Paz wear. Paz said she was twelve and too old for her animal dresses. I sat at the table on one side of Beto; Chloe sat on his other side.

"Your hair is very nice, Eliza," he said. He smelled great, like pine. I'd heard Forrest say there was such a thing as too much after-shave, but I wasn't so sure.

I felt funny in shorts. I wished Chloe hadn't talked me into wearing them. My knee touched Beto's under the table once, accidentally. I moved away, but he didn't seem to notice. Then I looked into the living room and saw Hector, wearing a party hat. The elastic string stretched under his beard, but he didn't seem to mind.

"Always he is invited to birthday parties," Paz said.

"He loves strawberry ice cream. Strawberries make goats dream good dreams."

"Where does he sleep?" Chloe said.

"His bed is now a coffin. Beto and my uncle Del made it for him," Paz said.

"He sleeps in a coffin?" I asked if we could see.

Beto, Paz, and Chloe and I walked out to the backyard, and they pointed to a long wooden box, turned on its side.

"It seems sad to sleep in a coffin," I said.

"Hector is not sad," Paz said.

"Still, it's spooky," Chloe said.

Beto shrugged. "What is the meaning of *spooky?*"

"You know, scary," she said.

"This feeling I do not understand about America," Beto said. "In Mexico we celebrate death."

"Celebrate it?" I said.

"Each year we feast and dress in costumes and dance in the streets. We call it Day of the Dead."

"Weird," Chloe said.

"Every year I miss it now," Paz said. "Especially the banana milk shakes."

Beto looked at me for the first time. "Paz has told me of your sister. I would like to know if her grave is in San Antonio?"

I paused. Since the day she was cremated, I'd tried not

to think about Holly's ashes. "I visit her gravesite whenever I can and take baby pink roses, her favorite."

Beto nodded.

Chloe stared at me, not blinking. She knew I was lying.

We followed Beto inside.

No one understood about Holly. Even after a whole year nothing was simple about it. It was like the words *flash flood, drowning,* and *ashes* were forbidden words. It was like we were ashamed of Holly. If I'd told the truth, I knew Beto and Paz would think my family didn't care enough to bury her.

After she'd been cremated, I'd never even had the nerve to ask where her ashes were. I'd always wished she had a real grave, so I could be alone with her.

Chloe wasn't speaking or even looking my way. I could feel what she was thinking through my whole body. All because a stupid lie had slipped out of my mouth like a wet cough drop. Sometimes lies did that. You didn't sense them coming.

□

Luna and Luz were seated across from me as Estrella set the cake down at Paz's place. Twelve candles.

Then the twelve candles turned into eleven. Holly was standing over her own birthday cake. Her hair swung forward on her face, and Mom brushed it back behind her ears. Holly held her breath and closed her eyes, then laughed and blew them out all at once. "I got my wish!" she yelled. I remember wondering what she might have wished for. She had everything.

Paz blew out all twelve candles, and everyone sang "Happy Birthday" to her. Except Chloe. She kept glancing at me, as if I were some stranger she'd just met. Estrella's voice filled the house. She served cake, and Hector ate more ice cream.

Then Estrella said it was time for the piñata. Beto blindfolded Paz and gave her a stick. Then she had to turn around ten times. She kept batting the air, while everyone laughed at her, until finally she split it open. Candy and plastic toys fell out everywhere. Paz and her cousins scrambled for them, but I just stood beside Beto and Chloe, as if I were too old for candy, even though I saw a Nestlé Crunch.

Beto asked Chloe if she'd seen the whooping cranes in Port Aransas yet. The radio was playing; I knew she couldn't hear.

"Whooping cranes," I said. "Have you seen them?"

"Never," she said to him. "I'd give anything to."

I just looked at her. She hated birds.

"One day soon at sunrise we will all go," he said. It wasn't even a question. He smiled at me. Chloe nodded.

I knew what Mom would say, but how could I say no again?

Estrella helped Paz try on her new dancing shoes, bronze with low heels. Paz couldn't stop looking at them. I remembered Holly's Oz shoes. She always said shoes could have big plans of their own.

Paz whispered in my ear that she felt too old for piñatas but didn't want to hurt her mother's feelings. Then I gave Paz her present, my "Don't Mess with Texas" T-shirt that I'd worn once to the pier dance. I knew she loved it. She ran into her room and came back out wearing it with jeans.

"You look so old tonight," I said.

Chloe looked at me, as though I were just saying it.

We said good night, but I didn't see Beto anywhere. Even though it was his sister's birthday, he'd left.

As we walked across the street, Chloe said, "Liza, you're lucky Holly couldn't hear what you said. That's all I have to say to you. I can't talk about this." She turned and ran in the direction of the beach.

All I could hear were crickets. I sat on the porch in the dark, feeling almost sick from too much cake. I knew it was more than just Chloe's usual dramatics. She was furious. But why should I apologize about what I chose to say or not say about my own sister? Was there some right way I was supposed to feel about Holly?

I could still hear the tone of her voice, sharp and soft at the same time, as though she'd made her mind up about me, forever. *You're lucky Holly couldn't hear what you said.*

"But you can, Holl," I said. My voice sounded deep, like it came from inside my pocket. I'd never told anyone, even Chloe, how I talked to Holly. How she answered me sometimes. Now I could hear her say, "Just where are those baby pink roses, Liza? I haven't seen one crummy rose from you yet."

I knew the conversations weren't real, but it made her feel close. Chloe wouldn't understand, and I'd never try to explain the way I might have in the past. I couldn't figure out exactly what seemed changed between Chloe and me. I wasn't sure if I had changed or if she had. Or maybe both.

c h a p t e r 9

I hadn't fallen asleep till almost two. I woke up late and heard voices. Chloe was still sleeping, so I crept downstairs.

Mom was sitting at the kitchen table, smiling. At Dad! She held her finger to her lips and pointed toward Mama Lacy's room. He came over and hugged me, as though it were just normal for him to drop in anytime.

"You did something different to your hair. I like it," he said.

"How come you're here?"

"Missed you. And your mother, of course." He glanced at Mom. Her makeup was fresh, and she wore Crushed Rose, her new lipstick. He didn't deserve it.

"Liza, I got up at the crack of dawn to drive down and surprise you. I'd like to take you and your mom out to breakfast. Is there an IHOP around? It used to be your favorite."

Why did he think he could just show up whenever he

wanted and think pancakes would make everything fine? He loved showing up as a "surprise." But after a while you got tired of it. His surprises were just a good way to avoid planning ahead.

"Chloe's here," I said.

Mom said, "There's an IHOP in Corpus. A perfect place to discuss issues. Chloe sleeps so late, anyway, that she won't miss you."

Dad winked at me. He hated issues.

"Are you selling the Willow house or not?" I said.

He looked at Mom. "That's up to your mother. There's nothing I want more than to have you both home again where you belong. I haven't put it on the market yet."

"We'll talk it over," Mom said in a whisper, nodding toward Mama Lacy's door.

"Why can't we talk now?"

"Liza," Dad said, "your mother's trying her best."

I just stood there. Maybe I wouldn't move from this spot until they told me something. That's what Holly would have done. She always made things happen the way she wanted.

Dad reached in his pocket, but Mom shook her head. Mama Lacy could smell cigarette smoke from China.

I went upstairs and got dressed quietly so Chloe could sleep. She used to say we were both night people, but ever since I'd been in Rockport, I kept waking up early; then

I'd be too tired to stay awake past ten. I hadn't told her yet that I might have changed types because she always said morning people were dull. Forrest said the whole day/night thing was just another Chloeism.

☐

Dad and I drove to Corpus along the coast road. Mom had a headache and decided at the last minute not to come. I figured it was a preconfab headache.

The bay was flat and gray like a puddle of oil. The pelicans skimmed the water. They couldn't seem to find a single fish.

Dad asked me how Chloe was.

"The same," I said. "Or almost."

"How about Forrest?"

"Okay."

"Have you heard from him?"

"Some."

"Absence makes the heart grow fonder. At least that's what I'm hoping happens with your mother. I think she's testing me this summer."

"I don't think absence makes the heart grow at all."

Dad opened his window and reached in his pocket for a cigarette. "I've wondered about it myself.

"It's hot with the window open."

He closed the window and reached across to turn up the air conditioner. His hands were tan. I still remembered how white his skin looked when I'd seen him through the skylight with Ms. Weller. My stomach felt queasy whenever I thought of it. Once right after Holly died, he'd told me, "You and your mother are my whole world." It seemed true for a while, but now I wasn't sure whether to believe him.

Finally he said, "I guess you've been lonesome down here, at least until Chloe arrived."

"It's smoky in here." I hated the way Dad thought we could be instant buddies.

He opened his window again. "Mama Lacy driving you crazy?"

"She's bossy and a racist," I said.

"I think that's a fair summation."

"She won't let me have friends over, and Mom won't stand up for me. She just keeps saying to wait till you come. That never happens."

He put out his cigarette. "It's not easy for either one of you, Liza. She asked me to come down today because she's worried about you. She thinks you haven't been yourself because you feel rejected by me. Is that true?"

I just looked at him. "Is the only reason you came down to discuss 'issues'?"

"No. Of course not. I've missed you terribly."

We drove the rest of the way without talking. I wondered if he really missed me. Maybe seeing me reminded him that he had only one daughter now. I wished I'd stayed with Chloe.

☐

Mom was wrong about IHOP; all we found was McDonald's. The place mats had stars for cities. I put my finger on San Antonio's star and made my usual wish.

Dad ordered only coffee even though he usually loved breakfast. I could tell he was nervous talking to me because he went outside and smoked two cigarettes in a row. I had a sausage Egg McMuffin and two hash browns. I remembered how I wasn't hungry for weeks after I saw him with Ms. Weller. Maybe it was finally his turn to be upset.

"You're mad at me, aren't you?" he said as he sat down.

Sometimes he sounded like a little kid in trouble. "You don't keep your promises. Nacho's spending his life at the kennel while you work."

He gazed into his coffee. "No, he's not. I haven't been gone that much. I'm going to be honest with you, Liza." He looked up.

"Wow. What an idea!"

"Watch the sarcasm. After I disappointed your mother by not coming down, she told me to stay away for a while and give you two some space. She said you were making friends. I've been trying to do what she says, even though it's hard as the devil. Maybe it looks to you like I don't care."

I finished my orange juice. "So the whole time you wanted to come and she wouldn't let you?"

He sighed. "You wouldn't talk to me on the phone, so I had no way of knowing how you felt. I figured maybe you'd gotten too busy to think about home." He hesitated. "Or me." He always blinked his eyes a lot when he was upset.

No matter how hard I tried with my family, I could never tell who was being honest with me, and when. "Mom tries to get everyone else to talk about feelings, but she won't be honest about her own. I don't have any idea if she's decided to stay in Rockport or what. I never know any facts in this family. I hate that!"

He put his cigarette out. "I guess I don't either, but it's not all her fault. You and I keep to ourselves quite a bit, too, and that makes it hard. At least your mom's trying."

We drove for a while, both looking straight ahead. Finally I said, "She's missing this confab."

He turned and smiled at me. I almost smiled back.

□

We got to Moonhaven just as Daddy Jake finished his breakfast. He was glad to see Dad, as usual. They always talked about basketball for a while, so I went out and walked around in the grape-colored hall.

Then I spotted the phone booth. I knew just hearing Forrest's voice would make me feel better. I decided to take a chance and call collect. His mother answered. She paused before accepting charges. I pictured her in her fuchsia warm-up suit with the pink sweatband creasing her leather forehead.

I told her I was calling from Rockport and would pay her back for my call. When she went to get Forrest, the phone clunked like she'd dropped it into the Grand Canyon.

Then I waited. Maybe she'd just forgotten about me. Finally I heard his voice, slowed down, like a cassette that was dragging. "Liza, is that you? Liza?"

"Are you okay? You sound sick."

"My allergies," he said. "I'm on some medicine that fogs my brain, so our trip to the canyon's been postponed. Mom's mad again."

"That's horrible. You know Chloe's here. Dad, too, finally."

"About time! Are you coming back with him?"

"If he wants. He hasn't said. It's kind of weird not to

know for sure if your own father wants you to come home with him. I wish people would just say what they mean. If I come, I'll bring Chloe. But she's not the same. It's hard to explain. Are you there, Forrest?''

''I'm here. I've been just sitting at my computer, tapping my feet, rereading your E-mail. It seems like about a year since you left.''

''It does?'' I started to say that it felt like that to me, too, but then I realized that it didn't. I'd been gone for five weeks, but for some reason it seemed shorter. ''I miss you,'' I said. That part was so true.

''My mom's motioning me to get off the phone,'' Forrest said. ''We have to go to the allergist.''

''I sent you a postcard of the pink crab,'' I said. ''Could you go to my backyard and tell Nacho I might be coming home?''

''I'll tell him,'' Forrest said.

☐

Dad was lying on Daddy Jake's bed, gazing at the water stain on the ceiling. ''Hi, honey.'' He said it really fast and in that too-cheerful way. Daddy Jake sat in his chair gazing out the window. I knew they'd been talking about Holly.

I wanted to talk about her, too. Not to cry about her.

Just to remember things together. At home Forrest would sit on the roof with me and remember how it was before she died. I'd told him how much I hated being the only child now.

"It's a responsibility," he'd said. "All your parents' dreams rest on your shoulders. I've had fourteen years' practice. You've had only one."

Dad was silent. He'd put on his sunglasses. We both cried easily and always needed to keep sunglasses close by, in case of emergencies. He went to the window and stood looking out toward the naval base. I knew he had been stationed there when he first met Mom. Now maybe he was wishing he'd never gotten married or had kids at all.

"Still got your foot doctor at home?" Daddy Jake said. I knew he was "making conversation" the way Mom sometimes did. He hardly ever did that.

I nodded.

"Tell him that the ostrich is the biggest bird of all, but he gets along fine with just two toes." Daddy Jake picked up his bird book. I looked over his shoulder. He was reading about the scissor-tailed flycatcher.

"Chloe's here visiting, Daddy Jake," I said. "I need to get back."

We told him good-bye. I promised to bring him home for supper next time we ran out of pork.

We drove back to Rockport without saying much. Dad kept the air-conditioning running full blast. It gave me chills. "Remember when Holly used to put her face in front of the vent and let her hair whip around her face?" I said.

Dad nodded. He remembered.

When we pulled up in front of the house, he turned off the engine. I knew he was either going to ask me now or make up an excuse why not. I kept my hand on the door handle, ready to jump out fast in case he had some lame excuse.

"Liza, come home with me for the weekend. Please?" His voice sounded urgent. He really wanted me home. Home!

"Can Chloe come?"

"I wouldn't have it any other way. Go pack a bag."

My stomach was already flipping around. I'd call Forrest as soon as I got home. "Great!" I said.

"Better than great," he said. "How about stupendous?" He reached over and hugged me. I knew we'd stop for lunch in Beeville and play Twenty Questions the whole way. He and I were always the best players in the family, but we hadn't played since Holly.

"I've missed the hell out of you, Liza," he said. "Go get Chloe and let's head home!"

□

Chlo was practicing. I turned off the cassette player and grabbed my backpack. "We're going to San Antonio with Dad for the weekend. He's waiting downstairs!"

She didn't answer.

"What's wrong?" She wasn't even taking off her toe shoes.

"I can't," she said.

"Why not?"

"I get carsick."

I just looked at her. "What do you mean? You never used to."

"Your dad drives that Jeep thing, right?"

"Chlo! I haven't gone home all summer. Now's my only chance. It's not a Jeep. It's a Ford Explorer."

"Go ahead without me if you want. You probably want to just hang with Forrest while you're there, anyhow." She shrugged as if she didn't care.

"Without you? I can't do that. This is our only time together all year. We can swim at the Willow pool, rent movies. I'll bake stuff. C'mon!"

"I'm telling you I get *carsick*," she said. She pushed the button and started the *Sleeping Beauty* tape again. She stretched her leg straight up in the air until it almost touched her shoulder.

"Maybe we could stop a lot along the way so you could rest?"

She put her leg down. "Liza, maybe life's just gotten too easy for you to see what it's like to be me."

"What do you mean?"

She sighed. "Your parents are together, you've lived in the same house all your life, you've got a boyfriend, even if it is Forrest, everyone likes you the second they meet you, plus you can *hear* what's going on. Believe me, you've got it made! Anyway, I get carsick, and I'm not going."

I couldn't even answer. She'd never once said in her whole life that she envied me. I didn't believe it. And I didn't believe the carsick story for one second either. It was something else. Maybe she wanted to stay near Beto.

"Okay. I'd rather stay here with you, anyway," I said, trying to sound as if I meant it. "I'll tell Dad to go on without us." I tried not to think how his freckled face would look when I told him. He'd think I was too busy for him. He wouldn't come down to Rockport again. I waited, hoping she'd change her mind.

She stretched the other leg to her shoulder. "Don't do anything on my account, Liza," she said. "You do what you want, and I'll do what I want. We're not Siamese twins, you know."

I wondered if she remembered. When we were in third grade, we used string to tie her left arm to my right arm and stayed like that all day to feel what it was like to be Siamese twins. Finally we'd both fallen asleep on her front porch, where her mom had found us, still tied together.

I headed downstairs to tell Dad. My feet felt heavy, as if they had weights on them. I thought of Chlo's arched foot in her pink toe shoe, raised high above her head. Then I thought of Forrest's foot on the floor beneath his computer, tapping out the seconds till I arrived. Why did you always end out choosing between the people you loved?

c h a p t e r 10

The flag was whipping around the pole in Mama Lacy's yard. That meant Mom had picked up Daddy Jake and brought him back from Moonhaven for dinner. He always put up the flag before he settled on the porch with his book.

"Wood larks sound like robins," he said.

"Daddy Jake, are you talking to me?"

"Whoever happens by. You'll do."

I sank down in the chair next to him. I decided not to talk about Chloe because it felt disloyal. "I've been wanting to tell you a secret of mine for a while," I said. "You know the Castillos, across the street? I might be in love with a whole family. Is that possible?"

"Well, once I fell in love with a whole species. Pigeons."

"Well, I wish I had a family where people didn't try to choose your friends for you and didn't ask what you were feeling and didn't break promises and make surprise visits and need space.''

"You left me off your blacklist," he said. "Thanks." He took off his glasses and sniffed. "What's your mom cooking in there? Gym socks?"

I decided not to let him humor me for once. "And I hate how Mama Lacy calls people wetbacks."

He nodded. "You're right. It's despicable. I've told her. Only seems to make her worse. But your grandmother's not mean-spirited, believe me. Just tough to understand. For one thing, she's got a broken heart to deal with these days."

"Do you mean Holly?"

He nodded.

"Still, it's not an excuse for her to get away with all she says," I said.

He took the handkerchief from his back pocket and polished his glasses. "You don't exactly treat her like the queen of Spain. Where's your bosom buddy?"

"Practicing." I remembered how Chloe and I always laughed at the word *bosom*. Sometimes we'd say it over and over and over, laughing until we'd finally collapse on the floor, screeching. We couldn't imagine that our bodies would ever actually grow one, let alone two, of anything gross enough to be called a *bosom*. "She's bored," I said.

"Why don't you ask somebody from the perfect family over here for dinner? Maybe you two need a fresh breeze."

Maybe he was right.

□

Mom was in the kitchen. "Could Paz come over for dinner?" I said. "She's home alone."

"I've overcooked the broccoli. All we've got is Mama's leftover soup. Maybe another time."

Mama Lacy looked up from the quiz show. "The Spanish child? Not in this house! They have different germs. Your grandfather's frail, picks up things. Your skin looks awful dry, Elizabeth Jane."

"What do you mean, different germs? Their house is cleaner than this one." I could feel my stomach tightening.

"You could eat off my kitchen floor," Mama Lacy said.

Mom wheeled Mama Lacy into the bathroom just as Chloe came downstairs.

I took Mama Lacy's silverware setting and place mat from the table, then went back for her plate, beer glass, and napkin. I set a place for Mama Lacy in the middle of the kitchen floor.

"What are you doing?" Chloe said.

When I told her, she started laughing.

Chlo and I sat down at the table. I counted six shreds of pork in my cabbage soup. It looked like dental floss. Once Mama Lacy had made peach cobbler for eight people out of one peach.

Mama Lacy got back from the bathroom and said, "Where's my place?"

"On the kitchen floor," I said. "It's cleaner there."

Chloe laughed. She was her old self.

"Girls, please!" Mom went to get Mama Lacy's supper off the floor.

Mama Lacy just sat there, looking down at the floor. "That's not one bit nice!" she said.

"You're not so nice lately yourself," Daddy Jake said.

"What do you mean?" Mama Lacy said.

"What's the harm in those folks across the street? They're Liza's friends. Maybe Número Uno needs something else to occupy her mind."

"Like what?"

"Like me."

She stopped eating her soup and looked at him.

I took my broccoli off my plate and put it in my napkin, so I could take it to Hector later for whatever ailed him.

Mom got up to get more lemon for the tea, then sat down and closed her eyes for a second. I missed Dad. He would have jumped up from the table right now and headed straight across the street to ask Paz over for dinner.

Mama Lacy said, "One thing I want to be real clear about is that I'm not partial to one race over another. It's just a matter of good breeding. Family generics."

"Genetics!" Daddy Jake said. "This is going too far. Cease!"

Mom pushed her chair back. "Liza. We'll talk about this later."

Chloe stood up and put her hands on her hips. "You know what? No one says what they mean in this house. I really hate that!"

No one spoke. She was right.

Then Chloe said, extra-loud, "You know what, Liza? Your grandmother's a racist!"

Mama Lacy put her spoon down and looked at Chloe, then at me. Her cheeks were creased like used tissue paper. She moved her soup bowl a few inches, then moved it back. She reached under the table and picked up Porky.

I stared at the bleached flowers on the tablecloth: hundreds of sprigs of lavender. I could almost smell Holly's cologne. I knew if she were here, none of this would have happened. She would have brought Paz home for dinner without even asking first. Then everyone would have loved Paz just because she was Holly's friend.

Mom said, "Chloe, I think you owe Mama an apology."

Mama Lacy was waiting. The corners of her mouth quivered, and I saw that her cheeks were wet. I handed her my paper napkin.

Chloe turned to me. "Why don't you say what you think, Liza? She's *your* grandmother."

I looked at Mama Lacy. When I was little, she could tell I was sick by laying her cheek against my arm. She'd always know if I had even one degree of fever.

Chloe was still waiting, but I didn't answer. Then she headed out the front door. I knew she expected me to follow her, but I didn't. I felt that if I looked at Mama Lacy's face one second longer, I'd end out saying Chloe didn't mean it, even though that would be a lie.

I headed upstairs to E-mail Forrest.

> *E-male*
> *Chloe called my grandmother a racist. She is one, so why do I feel sorry that Chloe said it?*
> *E-female*

When I went back downstairs, Chloe was still gone. Daddy Jake was sitting on the sofa, waiting for Mom to take him back to Moonhaven for the night. He was soaking his foot in a plastic tub. He wasn't even reading. Before I sat down, he said, "The right one puffed up on me. Looks like a strawberry Popsicle.'' He lifted his foot out of the water so I could see.

His toes were bigger than usual. The veins in his foot were buried so deep in the puffiness that I couldn't see them. ''Does it hurt a lot?''

''Can't remember when it didn't. Part of growing old.''

''Where's Mama Lacy?''

''Getting ready to go. Said she wanted to ride along when your mother takes me back to Moonhaven in a bit. I think she needs company tonight.''

''I know. Chloe shouldn't have said that.''

He studied his foot. ''What's done is done, Liza. I have a favor to ask you. I've got a friend at the retirement home named Delia Swann. Nice woman from Kentucky who plays bridge almost as good as Número Uno.'' He reached for his wallet.

''What about her?''

''Well, Sunday's her birthday, and I'd like to send her some nice flowers. I'll give you my credit card. Wait till we leave, then order a bouquet for her, something special. Feminine, like.''

''Something special?''

''Don't worry about price. She likes pink.''

I just looked at him. ''What about Mama Lacy?''

''What about her?''

"How would she like your sending flowers to a stranger?"

"Delia's no stranger. We've been friends a full year. Besides, Saturday she turns ninety. Think I'm in danger?" He handed me his credit card and went back to studying his foot.

I closed my eyes and fingered his credit card. The raised numbers felt like braille. I thought of Mama Lacy, by herself all year while Daddy Jake played bridge with Delia Swann.

I told him good night, but I didn't kiss him.

☐

I turned out the light and sat in the dark on my cot. Chloe still wasn't back. Mama Lacy had already turned off the air-conditioning for the night. My room was heating up to sauna status.

I tried to think of something I could do for Mama Lacy to make up for Chloe. I couldn't cook a whole dinner for her because she didn't like my "fancy food." There was no sense in baking a cake for her because she said no one did it like Sara Lee.

I could hear Mom and Mama Lacy and Daddy Jake going out the front door downstairs. I waited till I heard the car drive off, then headed for the kitchen to call the all-night florist. I told him to send a small bouquet of pink daisies to Delia Swann at Moonhaven Retirement Home, along with a Best Wishes card from Jake Lacy. Then I said to send a dozen yellow roses to Thelma Lacy on Raht Street. I told them the greeting card should read, ''Número Uno, always. Jake.''

c h a p t e r 11

I woke up early again, exhausted. I hadn't fallen asleep until late. I kept thinking about what Chloe had said. How Mama Lacy had reached to pick up Porky as if he were her only friend. I wanted to turn on the computer and E-mail Forrest, but Chloe was still asleep.

When I got downstairs, I put a piece of bread in the toaster. "Where's Mama Lacy?" I said.

"Still in bed. She's feeling pretty bad. Chloe certainly says what she thinks, doesn't she?"

"She's honest," I said. I hated the way I automatically jumped to defend Chloe. I needed to think first about what I really felt.

"Indeed," Mom said.

I buttered the toast. She handed me the honey and stood there watching. Mom seemed to be waiting for me to take sides. To feel sorry for Mama Lacy. I did feel sorry for her, but at least Chloe said what she thought. "When Chloe gets up, tell her I'm out for a walk." Like some boring morning person.

I wanted to talk to Dad, but the only phone was in the kitchen, where Mom was. I could almost hear his voice. "Buck up, Liza. Don't let Chloe get you down."

I headed for the beach. The sand felt warm under my feet as I walked along the edge of the water. I remembered when Mama Lacy and I used to go to the beach together. I loved the slits in her old white rubber bathing cap where her hair stuck through. It had red highlights then. She'd show me how the water would hold me up if I just lay on top and held my breath. She'd take her hand away a little bit at a time until I could barely tell if she was there at all. Then I was floating.

I kept walking and walking, not even thinking about where I was going. My feet knew just what direction to take. Then I realized I was at the lighthouse.

I climbed up to the top again, by myself this time. Chloe had said the lighthouse was boring, but I never once thought that. I thought it was peaceful and mysterious and lonely and not lonely, all at the same time. Sometimes when I did things with Chloe, I couldn't tell what I was feeling versus what she was feeling. As if our thoughts were still Siamese twins.

I stood at the top looking out at the bay. In a way I wished I could live up there forever. If you lived all by yourself in a lighthouse, you wouldn't ever have to think about anyone else's feelings.

I headed back toward Raht Street. My head felt clogged up with thoughts. The only person left to talk to was Paz. But then she'd have to find out Mama Lacy was a racist.

I needed someone.

□

Jennifer answered her door right away and asked me in. "Hi. You're Liza, right? I'm glad you finally came by." She wore a pink tennis skirt and matching top and said she'd just gotten back from a long tennis match. She still looked fresh. She'd obviously had practice at being a morning person.

We went to her bedroom, which was painted pale green, not a single picture on her wall. Just a wooden cross with tiny pearls on it, over her desk. She sat on the bed and motioned me to the rocker.

Suddenly I was sorry I'd come. Now I had to make small talk, the way Mom did, instead of talking about anything real. "Do you play tennis a lot?"

She nodded. "I hated it at first, but my dad's a coach,

so I've always played. Now I love it. What's wrong? You look upset.''

Now what? I didn't even know her. How could I talk to a complete stranger about Chloe? "I can't stay. Sorry," I said. I had to go before I said things I regretted.

"I'm not sorry," she said. "It's awful to be alone when you feel bad.''

Then it just came out. "My friend Chloe called my grandmother a racist.''

Jennifer's eyes widened. "She did? What a zinger! My dad's one, too, but I'd never have the nerve to say so.''

"Neither would I," I said. "Chloe has more nerve than anyone." I'd always been proud of Chloe's nerve, but now I wasn't sure. Even though she was right, it felt wrong. Chloe didn't always understand how complicated things were.

"My dad's on the city council. They're always trying to clear the illegals out. Once I went to the beach with a bunch of those kids. Dad said it was the 'wrong company' and wouldn't let me out of the house at night for two months. I never did that again.''

"What does your mom say?''

"She left last year because she couldn't stand how bigoted he is. I live with him because my mom drinks too much. Want to try my cookies?'' She went to get them.

I looked around her room. On the desk was a Senior Scout handbook, Sunday school newsletters, and a bunch of gold tennis trophies.

She came back with the cookies, oatmeal. "My mom used to make them better than I can."

"You must miss her."

She nodded. "Especially evenings. My dad's gone a lot. I guess that's why I like being around your grandmother. Last summer I kept seeing her out on her porch. Just sitting there in the dark. Then I heard your sister had died, and I went over to take her cookies and tell her I was sorry. That's when we first got to be friends. She showed me a ton of pictures of you. A whole album full."

"It was probably my sister. She thinks *you're* Mother Teresa."

Jennifer smiled.

I looked at her. She was beautiful, athletic. Religious and obedient, too. Even kind. Everything Mama Lacy would love. I needed a major overhaul.

"Why isn't your friend Chloe with you? I saw her. She's cute."

"I know. May I have another cookie? They're the best I've had since I left home."

She passed me the plate. "I co-edit the youth group

newsletter. Your grandmother said you're a writer. Maybe you'd write a guest column for me? Like what you think of Rockport so far or something.''

''She said that? I might, but what I think of Rockport might not be printable.''

She shrugged. ''Whatever. It's your opinion.''

''I need to get home. Chlo's probably awake by now. Thanks for the cookies. I'm kind of embarrassed I just showed up and unloaded on you.''

She gave me three cookies. ''Maybe I'll unload on you sometime. Give one to your grandmother and Chloe.''

''Thanks, Jennifer.'' We said good-bye. She was okay. She was more than okay. I didn't even regret telling her.

When I got home, Mom said Chloe was taking a bubble bath.

In the middle of the table were a dozen yellow roses with a gift card addressed to Mama Lacy.

I headed upstairs to check my E-mail:

E-female
Maybe your grandmother's not a racist. Just a bigot. I looked both words up in the dictionary.
A racist thinks her own race is better than everyone else's.
A bigot is rigidly devoted to her own group, religion, race, or politics and is intolerant of those who differ.

Your grandmother dislikes Mexicans, but doesn't she also dislike Catholics and Democrats and Chloe and pesto potatoes?
E-male

E-male
The girl next door is perfect. I really like her. Even my grandmother likes her. You might, too. She plays tennis and wins trophies.
E-female

I was starting to turn the computer off when I saw that Forrest had answered me already. He must have been sitting at his computer, tapping his foot.

E-female
When you say I might like your next-door neighbor, the tennis champ, I hope you say it facetiously. By the way, facetiously is the only word that has all the vowels, in order, including y. I miss you.
E-male

chapter 12

I made blueberry muffins from a mix and ate three with honey. Chlo had dry toast. "What do we do now?" she said. "Rockport is so boring. In Houston you never run out of stuff."

She went out to the porch, licking on a lemon half. Mom asked me if she was sick. Mama Lacy said Chloe was becoming apoplectic.

I said she wasn't *anorexic*. She was just moody. Once Chloe had told me all artists were naturally moody. I wondered if moody people just decided to become artists so later they'd have a good excuse.

Chloe had been sleeping late most days. Then we'd go swimming at the beach and walk the two miles to the lighthouse and back in the evening. She practiced twice a day. After dinner we'd walk to the town square for Slushees, then sit on the grass beside the pink crab, eating our cones.

"Did you know seventy-five percent of Americans are fat?" Chloe said. "In Rockport it must be ninety-nine percent! Look at those tourists!"

"No different from any other town," I said. I'd been worried that I might get fat myself because Estrella had brought fresh *buñuelos* over to Mama Lacy's house again. I'd eaten three for breakfast.

When we got back to the house, Chloe kept glancing across the street at the Castillos' driveway. I knew she missed Beto. He hadn't been back to work on the patio because he'd been helping his uncle Del fill an order for a large number of coffins. Paz was with him, so we hadn't seen her much either. They hadn't gone to the pier dance.

Chloe said she thought Paz was cute but awfully young and shy. She said Beto was adorable but too serious, like Forrest. She said she'd finally laid eyes on Jennifer Wells. "Too preppy" was all she said.

I just looked at Chloe. Maybe she was a bigot. She was "rigidly devoted to her own group": perfect, thin, vegetarian dancers who never told a lie.

□

I went out to the front porch. Chloe was licking her lemon half.

"Don't get mad when I say this, Liza, but you're not as

fun as you used to be. Since Holly, I mean.'' She looked away.

She'd never said anything like that to me ever before. I knew she couldn't possibly mean it. She was just in a bad mood. Still, I felt an ache in my throat and tears behind my eyes. I turned my face away so she wouldn't see. ''All you ever talk about is Houston. You never give me a chance.'' I realized I'd wanted to say that to her ever since she arrived.

She was pretending not to hear. ''Why don't you play your trombone anymore?''

''I quit. There's no marching band at Rockport High. I'm sure I'll still be here when school starts.''

''You mean, you're bagging the idea of going home?'' She got up and tossed her lemon in the trash can beside the porch.

I was starting to feel more mad than sad. ''What about you?'' I said. ''Didn't you move to Houston because your mom wanted to?''

''Houston's a lot better than Rockport.'' She sat on the porch rail and twisted her French braid around.

''Rockport's not that bad,'' I said.

We sat there not saying anything. I remembered how Chloe and I used to talk about every single detail of what we thought and felt. Now she kept things to herself even more than I did. She kept saying how fantastic her life was in Houston, but I didn't believe it anymore. Since she arrived, she hadn't even talked about my coming for a visit. Maybe she didn't want me to see what her life was really like. I knew she was lonely. And ashamed of being lonely, the way I used to be.

Mom came out on the porch. I'd never noticed before how she resembled Mama Lacy. Today she did. Her lipstick had worn off, and her hair hung around her face like shredded chicken. "Liza, I'm dropping Mama off at her hairdresser. Then I'll take you two to the beach over in Port Aransas. How does that sound?"

Chlo looked at me, waiting.

"Do you want to go to Port Aransas?" I asked.

"I can't sit out all day in the sun. My skin." She went inside for another lemon.

"How about if we go to a movie!" Mom said. "It'll be nice and cool inside." Mom was trying so hard, but she only liked family-type movies and always hid her eyes if there were bloody scenes. I'd made a vow to keep my eyes open my whole life no matter what happened, on-screen or off.

"No, thanks," I said. She just stood there disappointed. "I'd like to, Mom, but Chloe mostly likes Clint Eastwood."

"Are you two getting along all right?" she said.

I paused. I wondered how she knew. "She says I'm not as fun as I was, but she's not exactly the same either."

Mom sank down in the chair and laid her head back. "Nothing is." She sighed. I knew she'd been upstairs trying to work on her story on the computer, but she'd given up.

Mom talked about the sea air and time alone to heal, but it never happened. All she did was take Daddy Jake back and forth from Moonhaven, then take Mama Lacy on errands and doctors' appointments and to the beauty shop. Mama Lacy said getting her hair done lifted her spirits like nothing else. I was glad it lifted something because her hair was paralyzed.

Chloe let the screen door slam behind her. Then she collapsed on the porch in front of me and did her Mama Lacy impression. "Oh, my heart, my heart!"

"That's not how she does it," I said. "It's more like this." I patted my hand on my chest and made gasping sounds.

"Liza!" Mom said.

Then I heard something and turned around. Mama Lacy was watching from her wheelchair on the other side of the screen door. "Chloe's heart attack was boring," Mama Lacy said, "but yours was quite a thrill, Elizabeth Jane!"

"I'm sorry," I said. I could hear Holly saying, "That was really really dumb, Liza!"

Mama Lacy said, "I've got a proposition. Let's go down to the border tomorrow and shop if your mother's willing." Her voice sounded softer. She'd been in a good mood ever since she'd gotten the roses. I felt even worse about our heart attacks. Mama Lacy was being so incredibly nice.

Mom nodded.

"Great," Chloe said. "Time stopped ever since I came to Rockport!"

"I thought you got carsick?" I said.

"Not in Buicks."

Mama Lacy looked at me and rolled her eyes. I couldn't help but smile back. I went inside and brought her a Lone Star because I knew she always drank a beer in the afternoon. Then she asked me to get a dish so she could share it with Porky.

"Look at his fur," she said. "I think he's less matted already."

□

It was two hours to the Mexican border from Rockport. I'd made the trip before with Mama Lacy. She always bought "trinkets" and then bragged all the way back about her bargaining skills. She picked out baskets and souvenirs at the Mexican market that she didn't need. The next week she'd give it all to the Goodwill, which probably sold everything back to the Mexican market, where Mama Lacy would buy it next trip.

Just as we were leaving the house, Mama Lacy said, "Go next door and see if Jennifer's ready."

"What are you talking about?" I said.

"I asked her to go along," Mama Lacy said. "She never gets to do nice things like you do. We don't want to be selfish."

"What?" Chloe said.

"Jennifer," I said. "She's going with us."

Chloe rolled her eyes and whispered, "The Eagle Scout? Does the trip earn her a merit badge?"

☐

Chloe, Jennifer, and I sat in back. Mama Lacy was talking to Jennifer about the church youth group. She passed a bag of pork rinds back to us.

"No, thanks." Then Chloe whispered, "Those must be for dogs."

Jennifer said, "You can both go to youth group with me Sunday." She hadn't even let on that we'd already met. She was pretty cool.

Before I could answer, Mama Lacy said, "Going to church doesn't make you a Christian any more than going in the garage makes you a car."

136

Mom was humming "San Antonio Rose" while she drove. Lately she was humming more. I knew her conversations with Dad had been going better. When I'd talked to him last, he said he was "making progress" with Mom.

"What does that mean?" I said. "I like facts. Remember?"

"We haven't put the house on the market," he said. "That's a fact."

There was hope.

Mama Lacy sat up front and kept telling Mom to watch for cows in the road, even though Chloe reminded her twice that we weren't in Mexico yet.

As we approached the bridge at the border, Mama Lacy looked across the dry Rio Grande. "They just keep coming and coming and coming," she said in her loudest voice. She said her father once had a friend on the border patrol who would call in the middle of the night and ask for help. "No matter what time of night, my father stowed his rifle on the rack in his pickup and drove the three hours to the border. 'Sending wetbacks back where they belong' was the least he could do for his country, he always said."

"Enough, Mama!" Mom said. "We've been through this."

"I'm not staying in this car if she keeps that up," Chloe said.

"Well, they're only called wetbacks because they have to swim the Rio Grande to get here," Mama Lacy said, "unless somebody sneaks them over the border in a truck."

I thought of Beto's "secret business."

" 'Give us your tired, your poor,' " Jennifer said. She smiled at me.

"Not on my taxes!" Mama Lacy said.

"I'm turning around if this continues," Mom said.

"I'm hungry, but I don't want Mexican food," Chloe said.

"All food in Mexico is Mexican," Jennifer said.

"How about cross-cultural burritos for lunch?" Mom said. "I read about them in the *Rockport News*." She was always on the lookout for compromise plans.

Mama Lacy said we'd all get "Montezuma's revenge," but Mom convinced her when she said these burritos would be stuffed with cabbage and pork.

Mama Lacy ate two burritos and drank two Lone Stars. Chloe said everything was cooked in lard, so she'd just eat watermelon. As we strolled through the market, she whispered in my ear. "Let's lose the Scout!"

"Lose her?

"C'mon, Liza. Get real. She's a ditz. She'll be happier trinket shopping, anyway."

I looked at Jennifer. She had on a pink sundress with sandals, and her hair was loose on her tan shoulders. She looked nothing like a ditz and hadn't done anything to deserve this. I wanted to say no. Then I imagined the rest of the day. And the rest of the week. Chloe would clam up and treat me like a traitor, and this *was* Chloe's vacation. She hated sharing me, and I hadn't been the one to ask Jennifer along.

We waited until they were busy looking at dresses in the market, then slipped behind the gift shop out into the street. The sun beat down on my face, and the air felt so heavy I had to push it out of the way.

We headed for the gelato place that we'd seen just after we'd come over the bridge. The cute guy behind the counter couldn't stop looking at Chlo. He gave us free tastes and said the names of them in Spanish, then English. He was watching her heart-shaped mouth as she repeated the Spanish words after him.

I went outside to wait. I'd watched her flirt enough.

When I went back in, she was behind the counter with a handful of sample spoons, tasting every single sorbet. "Miguel told me to try them all," she said. "Then he wants to take me for a quick ride around the marketplace on his motorscooter. His shift's over."

"You can't. They're waiting for us," I said.

"Go ahead. I won't be long. He'll drop me off at the

market!'' She ran out the back of the store. I could hear her laugh. The rippling piano thing.

I ordered a scoop of Ooey Gooey Louie for myself and a scoop of passion fruit sorbet for Jennifer, then headed back. The ice cream melted fast. The only reason I'd gone along with Chloe was that we'd be together. How could she just leave like that?

Jennifer didn't even act upset. ''I told your mom that you two had an errand, a surprise present or something, just so they wouldn't worry. No problem.''

I gave Jennifer her half-melted cone. ''The whole thing was Chloe's idea,'' I said.

''Thanks. It's cool,'' she said. ''She's your old friend. They're the most important.''

''I'm not so sure. New ones are, too,'' I said.

She smiled. Then she told me about her new boyfriend, Joe Frank Richards, who coedited her newsletter.

I told her about Forrest. ''We've been E-mailing since I've been here,'' I said.

She said she'd just gotten her own E-mail address: ''Ten-Jen.''

Jennifer just kept getting better and better. Maybe I'd write that editorial for her newsletter.

When we got back, I E-mailed Forrest.

140

E-male
Chloe's got terminal boredom. How can I be to blame
for everything? Illegal immigrants and Eagle Scouts and
fat tourists and pork rinds.
                    E-female

chapter 13

The sun hadn't come up yet when Chloe and I sneaked across the street to the Castillos'. I took Mama Lacy's flashlight. The crickets in the cedar were still squawking, and I could feel mosquitoes nibbling on my arms. Chloe said Rockport smelled like dog's breath.

Chloe said she couldn't wait to see the whooping cranes. I didn't care anymore if I ever laid eyes on one. I just wanted to get back home before we were missed.

Beto waved as Paz got in back.

"I need to ride up front," Chloe said. "I get carsick real easy."

"Especially in trucks," I said. I climbed in back to keep Paz company.

Chloe wore shorts and a red halter top that I remembered from last year. Except now she was starting to fill it up. The disk jockey on the radio said the temperature was heading for the hundred-degree mark. "Dogs will be melting on the sidewalk," he said.

Beto opened the window between the cab and the back of the truck so Paz and I could hear the radio. I recognized the salsa beat. Beto let the truck coast out of the driveway before he started it. Maybe not to wake his mom.

Paz took my hand and smiled. "Liza, now is time I tell you something. You are worrying that he likes your friend better than you. I know this. You must not worry. He told me he is only kind to Chloe because she is your friend. My brother is not caring about any girl except one."

"What do you mean?"

She smiled. "Always Beto is going at night to Corpus Christi. It is a secret from my mother because he has no license to drive." She lowered her voice. "Beto has a girl-friend." She smiled and raised her eyebrows. "He already gives her his ring."

"A girlfriend!" His secret business was only a girlfriend. Chloe was still talking fast nonstop. She didn't know. He kept looking straight ahead at the road.

□

Behind Safeway the sun was coming up. It looked like a balloon full of orange juice. The road curved as we approached the ferry. The fishing boats were out, full force, and the bay glistened like blue sequins. The truest blue I'd ever seen. It was a magic blue. I wanted to buy a postcard of the bay and send it to Forrest. He needed some magic in his life.

The car ferry was rickety and needed paint, but I'd always loved it. It was called *The Little Shrimp* because it carried only twenty cars at a time. We parked on the lower deck and went upstairs to sit. The water made a shushing sound behind us.

I'd already told Beto I had to get home by noon before Mom decided to go upstairs and check why we were still asleep.

I watched Aransas Pass disappearing behind us, just as Port Aransas came into view ahead. I'd ridden the ferry a lot of times with Mama Lacy, but all she ever did was worry about Holly, who got seasick.

We were lucky to get seats in the stern because the boat was packed with people in swimsuits and shorts. One kid had a surfboard with a pink crab painted on it. Paz put on her Rollerblades and went to check out the rest of the boat. Beto told her to be careful not to fall overboard, but she said she was more used to Rollerblades than feet. I knew Forrest would say that was physically impossible.

After we'd docked, we drove off the boat and in five minutes got to the beach, packed with kids, mostly older. Radios blared.

Paz said she'd see us later and ran to play volleyball. I would have joined her so I wouldn't have to act as chaperone for Chloe, except I could never serve a volleyball without bruising my hand.

Chloe took off her shorts and T-shirt. She'd worn her unicorn bikini underneath, but Beto didn't seem to notice. I didn't bother to take off my cutoffs. I just wanted to spot one dumb crane and go home.

The wet sand felt cool under my feet as we walked along the edge of the water.

"It's hard to tell whooping cranes from sand cranes," Beto said.

"My grandfather says whooping cranes are more colorful," I said. Like a *National Geographic* reporter.

Chloe looked at me. I knew she couldn't hear because of the surf.

"I just said the whooping cranes are more colorful."

"These crowds!" Beto said. "No crane in his good mind would stay."

I knew he meant in his "right mind," but I didn't correct him because I liked the way he said it better. He talked about the different beaches in Mexico. "All white sand," he said. "My family went each Sunday for a picnic."

I'd never been on a family picnic. Once Mom had packed fried chicken and potato salad and angel cake for a Father's Day outing, but Dad forgot. Nacho had knocked the basket off the kitchen table and had a dog picnic.

We sat near the sand dunes. Chloe began talking nonstop about keeping in shape, rehearsals, recitals. Then Beto was talking about music. "Flamenco is the blues of Spain," he said. "You understand this word *blues?*"

Chloe couldn't hear. She gave me a blank look. I was tired of repeating.

Beto kept watching the sky for cranes.

Nobody said anything for a long time, but it wasn't the comfortable silence that I was used to with Forrest. Chloe looked antsy.

Beto watched the sky. Finally he said, "I want to know more of your family, Eliza."

I told him about the roof and Willow Street and Nacho.

Chloe went to the water's edge and started a sand castle. Either she couldn't hear or she was annoyed. I knew she wanted me to go over beside her, but all I wanted was to go home. To Willow Street. In a way I wanted Chloe to go home, too. To Houston. I wanted to stop worrying every moment about what she was thinking and how she couldn't hear things and how bad she felt. Most of all, I wanted to stop feeling that I had to make the world all right for her.

Beto lay on his towel for a while and closed his eyes.

Chloe rubbed suntan lotion on her legs and arms, glancing at Beto to see if he was watching.

When he finally sat up, I said, "No cranes."

"No," Beto said. "Now is time to go home."

☐

Paz was asleep beside me in the back of the truck. I could already feel my sunburn heating up on my face. Beto stopped at a red light and opened a thermos of lemonade. He passed the cup back to me through the open window in the cab. Chloe was still up front beside him.

"Can I drive for just a little while?" She said it in her saloon voice. On Willow Street we'd both worked on deepening our voices by smoking her mom's French cigarettes. Mine hadn't improved much, but she always said that hers had. I couldn't tell.

Beto shook his head. "Your driving is not an idea that is good."

"I almost have my permit. I drive in Houston all the time," Chloe said. "Traffic here is nothing." She smiled and tossed her hair.

Beto told her no, but then he laughed. Chloe asked again, lowering her voice even more. I could see her profile, one dimple showing. She did look like Meg Ryan. Forrest even said so once.

"For a short while only you drive," Beto said. "Very slow to the corner."

"I drive best barefoot," Chloe said as she got behind the wheel.

She killed the engine and restarted it. "This truck is too heavy for you," he said. "Better I drive."

"I'm fine," she said. The truck chugged ahead.

"Just two blocks to the town square," he said. "Then I will drive."

Paz woke up and couldn't believe he was letting Chloe take the wheel.

"It's hard to say no to her," I whispered. I didn't feel mad. Just scared. I knew she could barely drive.

Chloe turned the radio full blast. "Oh, let me just go around the crab once?"

"Stop the truck," Beto said.

Chloe sped up.

"She goes too fast," Paz said.

"Let's have fun," Chloe said. "There's no cars around. Once around the crab, and I'll stop." She entered the town square.

"Stop," Beto said. "Please!"

Maybe she didn't hear. We kept heading toward the crab.

Beto said, "Watch out. Stop!" The truck jolted, and Beto tried to grab the wheel. Paz screamed. The truck jumped the curb, sped over the grass, and smashed into the pink crab.

"Oh, God," Chloe said.

We'd landed at a tilt. Salsa still blared from the radio. Paz was sobbing.

Beto got behind the wheel and tried backing off the crab. The engine just roared, but we didn't move. He tried again and again. "This is not good," he said. He kept looking in his rearview mirror. "Not good!" he repeated. Paz was still crying beside me.

Beto closed his eyes and sat there a moment, gripping the wheel. Then he raised his voice. "Paz, we must go now. You understand. Right *now!*" He glanced at me. "I am sorry, Eliza." He opened the door and held out his hand to Paz, so she could jump down to the ground. Then he said, "Let's go!"

Then they were running. Straight down Water Street, turning toward Raht. He was still holding on to her hand, and she was barely keeping up. They disappeared around the corner.

Chloe turned and looked at me. "What's happening?" she said.

I climbed up beside her into the driver's seat.

"My God!" she said. "How could they leave like that? Liza! What's happening?"

"Because they're *illegals!* That's why. They're scared."

"Aliens? Liza, I can't believe you didn't tell me that before!"

"Chloe, they're not creatures from outer space. The reason I didn't tell you is that I knew you'd get like this. Anyway, listen! When the sheriff comes, we're going to tell him that we borrowed this truck from our neighbor's driveway. Do you understand? *I* was driving. We're not even going to mention that Beto and Paz were with us at all."

She was already shaking her head. "No way, Liza," she said. "Not me. Not this kid."

"What do mean, no way? We'll get into some trouble, probably just grounded or something, but nothing like what can happen to *them*. We just can't involve them, that's all, or they'll be in big trouble. Say you understand!"

She shook head. "Maybe you've been away from me so long that you forgot. I'm not someone who lies to protect people. I tell the truth."

I heard the siren. "You can't. Please, Chloe, we've *got* to do the right thing for them. We have to stick together."

She wouldn't look at me.

A police car was pulling up behind us.

The chubby officer got out of his car. He was chewing gum as he came up beside my window. "You ladies all right?" he said. He leaned on the car and looked at me, then at Chloe. "I'm Sheriff Bobele. Little problem here? Driver's license?"

I shook my head, then told him the story.

When I finished, he glanced at Chloe, who spoke before he even asked her anything. "She wasn't driving," Chloe said. "I was. The boy who let me drive his truck just ran off down the street," she said. "I drove for only a few blocks. I didn't know he was illegal until just now, or I wouldn't have been in the car with him! I'm sorry."

"Chloe!" I yelled.

She glanced at me, her eyes wide, as if she had no idea why I was upset.

The sheriff went around to Chloe's side and questioned her, gently, mostly about where Beto lived, how old he was, how long she'd known him. Then he raised his eyebrows and asked if her version was the right one. He knew. I had no choice. I nodded.

I knew wherever Beto and Paz were now, they were wishing they'd never met either one of us.

"I'm taking you ladies on home where you belong," the sheriff said.

We sat together behind him.

"Look at the back of his neck," Chloe whispered. "It's like melting scoops of ice cream."

"That's not funny," I said. I moved to the far side. I didn't even want to be next to her.

"Where do you ladies live?" the sheriff said.

"Could you not call us ladies?" Chloe said.

He turned around and winked at her. "Sorry. Slip of the tongue."

"Twenty-seven Raht Street," I said. I looked back through the rear window and saw the tow truck pulling up.

I glanced at Chloe, who was leaning forward to talk to the officer. In spite of all the damage she'd done, she still felt pure for telling the truth. Now she was chatting nonstop about traffic in Houston.

We stopped in front of Mama Lacy's house. I could see Mom standing on the porch beside Mama Lacy, who had her hand on her chest.

Then Mom came running across the lawn. "Liza!" Mom said, putting her arms around me. "What on earth? Are you all right?"

I fixed pasta and marinara sauce. Mama Lacy and Daddy Jake stayed out on the porch, talking. More roses for Mama Lacy were on the kitchen table. Red. Daddy Jake had liked my idea when I told him. Now he'd sent his own!

Mom had called Dad, then put me on the phone so he could do the yelling. "How could you sneak out like that? You could have been seriously hurt! Dammit, Liza!"

Mom asked me to fix dinner. She said she simply couldn't take any more tension and went to her room.

Mama Lacy said it all sounded like "funny business" to her.

Chloe was slicing tomatoes. She kept saying she couldn't even talk about the accident and was glad she'd decided to leave tomorrow. She lowered her voice. "You shouldn't have lied."

"I thought you couldn't talk about the accident." I set the pasta marinara on the table so hard it almost spilled.

Daddy Jake brought Mama Lacy to the table from the front porch, and we all sat down. Mama Lacy's hands rested on the chrome arms of the wheelchair. The end of her index finger was blunt, squared off where she'd cut off the tip of her finger. For some reason I felt like touching it.

Mama Lacy said, "Never did care much for McNamara sauce."

"Marinara!" Daddy Jake said. He picked up his book and read out loud about how hummingbirds can fly upside down and backward while they flutter their wings eighty times a second.

Mama Lacy asked Chloe something. I knew she'd heard, but she didn't answer. After about two bites of food she pushed her chair back and went to take a bath.

"What's eating her?" Daddy Jake said.

"The funny business," Mama Lacy said.

"Maybe she has a guilty conscience," I said. "She ought to."

Daddy Jake shook his head. "Don't bet on it."

"Lucky if she has a conscience at all, let alone a guilty one," Mama Lacy said.

They sat at the table drinking coffee while I did the dishes. I liked seeing them there together, talking and whispering the way they used to. I could hear Chloe's bathwater, still running.

"She's using up all the hot water," Mama Lacy said.

Daddy Jake said, "I guess I'll just get back to the haven pretty soon."

"What's the hurry, Jake?" Mama Lacy said.

"You're right," he said. "Time's same here as there. Like the farmer who held a pig up to a fruit tree so it could eat some apricots. A guy came by and told him it'd save time if he shook the tree first, then let the pig just eat the fruit off the ground. The farmer said, 'What's time to a pig?'"

Mama Lacy was laughing. I kissed Daddy Jake good night. Then I leaned over and kissed Mama Lacy on the cheek.

"Thank you kindly, Liza," she said.

I was halfway upstairs before I realized she'd called me Liza.

☐

I was already in my cot. My whole body felt stiff, as if someone had tied all my muscles together in knots. Chloe came upstairs to blow-dry her hair. She sat on the floor, beside the plug, holding her head upside down and running her fingers through the long strands, over and over. As if her silky hair mattered more than the life of a whole family.

When she finished, she turned off the light and got in bed. "It's hot in here."

I threw back my sheet and got up to open the window. Then I stood there, watching the light from the lighthouse flash on and off, breaking the darkness into halves. I had to say more.

"Chloe, you might have ruined everything for them."

"I can't hear you," she said.

I turned on the light and sat on her cot so she could read my lips. I explained about Paz's medical treatment. How they'd sacrificed for her, coming without their father to Texas.

She interrupted. "They didn't tell the truth!" she said.

"You sound like a broken record. Things aren't so simple. I can't trust you to keep a secret. I never could!"

She sat up, pulling the sheet around her shoulders. "What do you mean, you can't trust me? You don't mean it." Her green eyes widened. "Are you saying you've kept other secrets from me?"

I wanted to tell her about Dad. She was still living across the street from me when it had happened, but I'd never told her about his affair with Ms. Weller. I knew she'd insist that Mom know the truth and might even tell her.

She gripped her sheet to her chest. Her knuckles were white from holding on. She glared at me, waiting for me to say something more. Or to take it back.

My legs felt weak and mushy as I got up, but I couldn't sit there any longer. Maybe I didn't have any more to say.

Then she said, "Okay. I get it. I understand. Maybe I've been dense, but now I get it, Liza. You don't want to be friends anymore. You've got Forrest and plenty of other people, so . . ." She began stripping the bed. Her heart-shaped lips were sewn together, a straight seam. I could imagine her old, like Mama Lacy. Disappointed with everyone.

"You're still thinking about yourself," I said. "What about them? Don't you see?" Why was I explaining, pleading? It was time to stop.

She held her bedding in front of her, like armor. "Liza, just because you like that family doesn't mean you have to go along with everything they do."

I looked at her. She had no idea how long I'd been going along with her every wish, even when I disagreed. I said, "You knew the real reason you were moving to Houston was your parents' divorce, but you kept their secret all year."

"That's because they asked me to," she said.

"Good reason," I said. "There're lots of good reasons.

That's what I've been trying to say. Some things are more important than the truth!'' Those words sounded familiar. Then I remembered. The volleyball voice.

Chloe put her hands on her hips. "What things? Give me a for instance, Liza!"

"For instance, kindness," I said.

She looked at me puzzled, waiting for me to say something more. All my life she was always waiting for me to help her understand. To make her laugh. To make everything all right.

I couldn't do it anymore.

She put her bedding down and began folding each blanket into a perfect square, concentrating on smoothing out the wrinkles.

I went to my cot and got in.

She picked up her pillow and blankets, then hesitated at the top of the stairs.

"Turn off the light!" I said.

□

I'd been in bed a long time, listening to foghorns from the bay. I held my hands up in front of my face and moved them around. In the dark they looked like someone else's, not even attached to me. It wasn't a scary feeling exactly, just strange. I didn't feel that ache all over my body the way I used to after a fight with Chloe. I didn't feel sad either. It was a floaty feeling. Part of myself had just gone off somewhere without me.

I finally heard Mom's footsteps. She sat on the edge of my cot, but I stayed on my side with my face turned away. If she knew I was awake, I'd have to talk. I'd already told her the facts about the accident, but now I knew she wanted to talk about feelings.

"Liza, turn over, please. I know you're awake." Her voice was strong.

I peeled a tiny silver of paint off the wall.

Then she put her hand under my nightshirt and rubbed my back. "We need to talk, Liza. It's silly for us to stay in our separate rooms, feeling awful. I know you and Chloe had a terrible fight. I could hear the yelling."

I knew Mom wanted me to tell her everything, but as soon as I put words on what I felt, I knew my feelings would change into something else. Like putting Jell-O into a mold. I wanted to understand first.

Mom said, "I don't understand why you sneaked out like that. Don't you know by now that you can tell me things? Confide in me?"

I turned over. "You don't tell *me* things," I said. "You told Dad to stay away from Rockport. I thought he didn't even care."

She paused. "Oh, darling, I know. I just knew you'd be so upset with me."

"Mom! That's why I don't tell you things. Because I don't want to upset you. I hate sneaking around, but you're so afraid of everything. Since Holly died, all you do is worry."

Her hand stayed on my back, not moving. I'd brought up the forbidden subject. Finally she said, "I know." Then in a whisper: "I'm trying to stop, honest. But you're not helping much."

We were quiet a long while.

I looked hard at her. I wanted to talk about Chloe, but it felt like too much effort to find the words. If only people could climb inside each other's brains and pick around for what they needed.

I turned back toward the wall and peeled more slivers of paint. It felt good, like peeling flakes off your skin after a bad sunburn. She started rubbing my back again, a soft tickle like a feather. "It's awfully warm up here," she said. "I don't know how you sleep."

Maybe this talk was too much effort for her, too. Still, I loved having her there beside me. I wanted to say something, anything, so she wouldn't go away. I thought of all the times this summer I'd hurt her feelings. How she kept on forgiving me. Just as she kept on forgiving Mama Lacy and Dad.

"Mom?"

"Hmm?"

"How do you keep on forgiving somebody when they never forgive you back?"

She didn't answer.

"Mom?"

"Your questions are getting too hard, Liza. I guess I don't know the answer, but sometimes you simply know when you reach your limits. Thanks for asking me, anyway."

She started to say good night, but I reached for her arm. "I wrote an editorial for Jennifer's newsletter," I said, "but now I'm not sure I should give it to her. I even included a multiple-choice quiz, so people could figure out if they were a bigot or a racist."

She laughed. "Oh, Liza. Let me tell you something that you may not have thought about. Mama didn't need that brick patio out back in such a hurry. Did you ever consider that? She managed to get along without one for forty years."

"What do you mean?"

"Well, she hired Beto for that job because he was your friend. She said she felt bad about some things she'd said to you about the Castillos."

"Why didn't she just tell me?"

Mom laughed. "Have you ever noticed, Liza, that saying what you feel is often harder than it seems?"

I touched her wrist. She was wearing the friendship bracelet that Holly had woven for her at summer camp.

She went on. "I suppose the patio was Mama's way of apologizing. She's never known how to say she's wrong about anything. Besides, it's tough for her in this community with everyone so set in their ways. Sometimes she just goes along with them."

"So she let Beto build a patio?"

Mom laughed. "She loves you very much, even if that's an odd way of showing it. And she spent hours on that photo album. Did you even glance at it?"

I shook my head.

Mom went on. "You don't go out of your way to show that you care for her either. She suggested the trip to the border with Jennifer; then you ran off with Chloe." She smoothed my hair.

How could she keep on loving me? I didn't deserve it. "I know," I said.

She paused. "I honestly don't know what to do about this move to Rockport. I feel pulled between you and Mama and your father. I love you all so very much." Her voice sounded strong. "We'll just see."

I waited for her to talk more about the plans, but she didn't. I knew she'd made up her mind to move. She just didn't want to say. Maybe she and Dad wanted to tell me together.

"Tonight I was counting all the things I'm sorry for this summer," Mom said. "I got to seventeen and was still counting when I heard you up here fighting. It's one more thing I'm sorry about. You two girls. Even though it was inevitable. You two were growing in different directions."

"Inevitable?" I said.

She kissed me. "Enough now," she said.

I lay there awhile after she left. Inevitable. It was a Forrest word. Five vowels.

I sneaked downstairs past Chloe, asleep on the sofa. Her hair was spread across the pillow, just her legs covered. She looked like the Little Mermaid.

I unplugged the phone from the kitchen wall, carried it upstairs and dialed Forrest. Even though it was after midnight, I knew I had to hear his voice before I turned out the light.

His mother answered on the first ring. "He's asleep," she said. "Call back tomorrow."

"I need to talk to him now, Ms. Schloss," I said. "It's an emergency."

She paused, then said she'd go wake him. I could hear

Forrest's father growling in the background. Or maybe it was one of their German shepherds that slept on their bed.

After a minute Forrest picked up the extension. "Liza?" he said. "Are you okay?"

I paused. Then I said it. "Chloe and I aren't friends anymore, Forrest." My voice came out louder than I expected. I could hear it echoing inside my head. It felt more real when I said it aloud, like a fact instead of a dream. I remembered all the New Year's Eves with Chloe when we'd climb onto my roof to renew our sacred vow. "No matter what happens," we'd say, "forever together."

"Jeez, Liza." We were quiet for a moment. Then he said, "I was afraid this might happen someday."

"You were?"

He paused. "Chloe's always needed you more than you needed her."

I didn't answer at first. Then I said, "I think it *used* to be the other way around."

"Maybe, but one thing I'm sure of is that there's nothing you can do to change her."

I knew he was right. "Mom said it was inevitable."

"Good word."

We were quiet. Finally I said, "Are you still there?"

"I'm here."

I needed to tell him now. *We're probably not coming*

home. I could feel the words tickling my tongue; then I swallowed them. I didn't need to tell him quite yet. Just hearing him was enough. "I'm really sorry I woke you and your parents."

"I'm not," he said. "I was dreaming about you, anyway."

"You were?" Forrest didn't ever talk about his dreams.

"You and I were in an elevator together and wanted to get to the second floor. Someone told us to ride up five floors and then down three. I asked why we couldn't just ride up two in the first place. They said that was the scientific way, but smart people like us always took the unscientific way."

"Weird dream," I said. "Did we get there?"

"I don't know. You woke me on the fourth floor."

I told Forrest to go back to sleep and continue his dream. "Let me know if we ever get off the elevator," I said.

E-female
You're still the only girl I can talk to.
E-male

Lightning flashed from the direction of Corpus. Somebody else's thunderstorm. I headed across the street to Candy Land. The sky had darkened, and the clouds looked like bruises.

I went around back. No Hector in the yard. The broken burro piñata lay on the back step next to Paz's Rollerblades. Then I saw the note pinned to them.

> *Eliza, these are for you. I hope they fit. You be careful at first that you don't hurt your knees. Here is my box of Band-Aids. We gave Hector to a farmer who grows strawberries, so Hector will have good dreams always.*
>
> > *Paz*

I sat down on the step. My body felt like a boulder. Like it wouldn't move again, ever. They were gone. Sometime during the night they'd decided to leave Rockport before the sheriff found them.

I imagined Estrella in the dark, packing her hair dryers, her gels, and her purple curlers.

I imagined Paz's tiny feet, without Rollerblades, following Beto and Estrella down Raht Street, knowing that she might not ever grow taller. Forrest said your feet were your bravest part, but I didn't believe it. If she never got her growth hormones, then every single part of her body would have to be brave.

I looked into their kitchen window. No string of peppers. Estrella's tortilla pan was gone from its hook. I could almost smell Paz's *limón* hair spray.

Maybe they'd gone to Houston to be closer to Paz's doctors. Or back to Guadalajara to be with their father. Wherever they were, at least I knew they were safe. They were a family.

☐

We rode in silence to the bus station. Mom suggested Chloe and I sit in back together. But we didn't have anything left to say.

I decided to tell her. "Beto and Paz are gone," I said.

"The whole family left in the night, before the sheriff could send them back to Mexico."

She didn't answer. Maybe she was feeling some regret. Or else she didn't hear. Then she said, "Well, what do you expect? They were dishonest people." She gazed out the window.

"They're not dead! They're just somewhere else."

She shook her head. "Don't freak out!" she said.

I hated the way she used those cool phrases. "I'm not. You obviously don't care about anyone but yourself."

She didn't answer.

I helped her carry her suitcases inside the bus station. She said not to wait, but Mom said we would, anyway, because bus stations weren't good places to be alone. Chloe raised her eyebrows when Mom said that. She'd already told me a hundred times I should cut the umbilical cord. Once she said, "The day will come, Liza, when you won't hear your parents' voices inside your head every time you go to make a decision." I tried to imagine.

Mom drank coffee and read the paper, while Chloe and I stood by the bulletin board. Chloe read the signs about yard sales, but I knew it was so she wouldn't have to talk. There used to never be enough minutes to say all we had to say to each other. We'd practiced saloon songs so many hours in her emerald room. Her dog, Lilac, and all the stuffed lions had listened from the window seat. I remembered our duet, "Is That All There Is?" Chloe could sing it even better than Peggy Lee.

I looked at her profile. Her nose was the best nose in the whole world. Small and straight. She held her head high, as if she didn't have a single worry. But I knew she did. She was lonely and couldn't talk about it. I was her only friend, and now she'd lost *me*. She'd have to find someone else who thought she was perfect, someone who would put up with her moods, tantrums, and demands and always be the one to apologize. And if she found someone like that again, how long would it last?

Finally the bus pulled up outside. It was starting to rain. Mom hugged Chloe, then left us alone to say good-bye.

Chloe looked up at the sky. I remembered lying on the front grass with her in San Antonio when we were little. We'd gaze at the sky through the sycamore leaves and try to imagine ourselves as old. Fifteen, twenty, thirty years old. We could never get to forty without laughing.

She started up the bus stairs, then turned around. She bit her lip. She hated more than anything to cry in public. Her hair was gathering raindrops all over, like sparkles. I wanted to reach out and smooth the water away.

"Did you get your ballet case?" I said.

She didn't hear me, so I had to repeat.

She nodded, then climbed to the top stair and hesitated.

"Does your mom know what time you arrive?" I said, louder.

She nodded and gave her ticket to the driver. Then she made her way down the aisle of the bus. I waited for her to find a seat on the side closest to me so we could wave. When we were little, she used to push her face up against the rear window of her car when she was leaving for vacation. She'd squish her tiny nose flat so she looked like Miss Piggy.

She went to the far side of the bus, where I couldn't see her. The rain was coming down harder, soaking me, but I didn't care. I hurried around the front to find her on the other side. Then the bus made a roaring sound, just as it started to pull away. A blast of fumes hit my face.

I closed my eyes a second, but when I opened them, the bus was already disappearing around the corner. A dot of gray moving off down Water Street.

chapter 16

The electricity was out from the storm. It wasn't even noon, but the kitchen was still dark as a tomb. I looked out the window into the backyard and saw Beto's pile of bricks, waiting. Mama Lacy had only half a patio.

In the middle of the kitchen table was a box of chocolates, with a card that read, "For Número Uno. Jake." I picked a dark chocolate truffle, my favorite, and ate it in two bites. Then I had another. Raspberry cream.

Mom had wanted me to go to lunch with them at Moonhaven, but I'd told her I needed to be alone. She understood. I hadn't been hungry, but now I felt hungrier than I'd ever felt in my whole life.

I opened the refrigerator: a jar of bacon drippings, pickles, mayonnaise, ketchup, prunes, leftover sauerkraut. The house was quiet except for the dripping faucet. Usually I loved having the house to myself, but now it seemed like a mortuary. I missed Nacho. He could always tell when I was upset.

I took out the bowl of Chloe's leftover tofu from the refrigerator. It wiggled as if it were alive. I got a spoon and took a taste, feeling it slide down my throat, disappearing as if I hadn't eaten it at all. I took another bite, then another until it was gone. The smoothness in my mouth almost made me cry. I put the bowl in the sink.

Then I ate Chloe's carrot sticks, one by one, out of the Baggies, even though I'd never liked carrot sticks. They snapped and echoed inside my head. The whole empty house could hear. Then her leftover carob. Mounds of brown mush, so sweet it made my face hurt. I drank some of her grapefruit juice, unsweetened, out of the bottle.

Then I saw the avocado we hadn't eaten, the huge one I'd found at Safeway. Soft and overripe now, perfect for guacamole. I stood over the sink, peeling off the leathery skin. Inside, the green was almost the color of Chloe's eyes. I took a knife and cut a thin slice, slipping it into my mouth. It almost dissolved by itself. Then I cut another slice, and another, and another. Finally I put the knife down and ate the rest, all the way down to the pit. The nutty smoothness made my eyes water. It was the best thing I'd ever eaten.

I placed the pit in a glass of water, the way I'd seen Mom do, so it would root someday.

☐

My room in the roof was hot because the air-conditioning had cut off with the storm. Black clouds had gathered over the bay, making it gray instead of sequin blue. I stood looking out the dormer window at the lighthouse. A little bit of sun came through the clouds and made it look white and sparkling again.

The light flashed. I closed my eyes and counted eight seconds. It flashed again. When I was little, I used to think the lighthouse would flash forever.

I began packing. Bathing suit, shorts. All I'd need for my backpack. Enough for one week.

On top of my suitcase I found the photo of Chloe and me dressed in old-fashioned clothes. We thought we looked so old that summer. Her hand rested on my shoulder, as if she owned me. In the lower corner of each other's pictures we'd signed our names in emerald green ink, her favorite color. I touched the words she'd written on mine, in her perfect round handwriting. "Heart/heart. Forever together." Then I wrapped the photo in tissue paper and placed it in the bottom of my suitcase.

I headed down to write my note:

Dear Mom,

    I'm taking a bus back home. Don't worry. I'll be back in a week, in time to start school in Rockport.

    Love, Liza

    I left the note on the kitchen beside Mama Lacy's photo album, the one she'd told me at least ten times to take a look at. I knew Mom had left it out so I'd see it. I opened it. Inside the cover it read, ''This belongs to Thelma Lacy and Liza Brody.''

    I didn't remember seeing most of the photos before. Me in a blue Easter dress. Me at the Willow Street pool, with Forrest. Me with Nacho in the front yard. Me and Chloe, roller-skating on the sidewalk. Me and Mama Lacy playing gin rummy on her porch. Me in my nightshirt on the roof. Me in my new dress for the Valentine Dance. There was even one of me and Mama Lacy on the beach, skipping. She used to say that skipping was a perfectly acceptable form of transportation for anyone, even adults.

    Suddenly the pictures got blurry. Mama Lacy had remembered me.

    I decided to add to my note:

    P.S. Mama Lacy—I hope it's okay that I ate some of your candy. I LOVE our photo album.

It started to rain as I walked to the bus station. On the Greyhound bus I sat across the aisle from a skinny kid with a headset who kept snapping his fingers to music I couldn't hear. He was living life between his ears.

Rain drizzled in curly streams down the bus window, and I could see my reflection. My hair was a messy, round, kinky mushroom, but I liked it. I remembered Chloe saying, "You look just like a Paris model, Liza!"

No one sat in the seat next to me, so I pulled the armrest up and stretched across the two seats. Then I slept almost the whole way, three hours. It wasn't a jerky kind of sleep but the slow, melting kind. In my bones and muscles I was already back on Willow Street.

The bus driver called, "Beeville!" Some people got off. Then I fell back asleep.

I dreamed Daddy Jake and I were racing bees. We put red tags on their stingers, so we'd know which bee got back to the hive first. We weren't afraid of them because we'd raced them so long they were like family.

I was tasting honey when the bus driver called out, "San Antonio!"

The bus station was a long way from Willow, and it was late. But that was okay. I pictured Chloe getting off her bus in Houston, meeting Gabrielle, telling her what had happened to us. "Liza just wasn't the same!" she'd say.

Maybe she was right. And maybe *that* was okay, too. One thing about me was the same: I'd always love her.

I had enough money for a taxi but figured I'd save and take the city bus. I always liked riding VIA. It meant "The Way" in Spanish.

I waited beside the Doloroso Bridge. The river walk was lit up with colored lights, and the riverboats were packed with tourists making their way down the river to La Villita, where the artists sold their crafts.

The clouds overhead looked like meringue. I stood in the shade of a mimosa that had dropped its lacy blooms all over the sidewalk. It smelled like vanilla.

VIA wound past the Alamo, past Hemisphere Tower, where the restaurant on top revolved so everyone could view the city. Once when we'd gone there for dinner, Holly had said she was seasick. She'd begged Dad to demand his money back.

For a moment I couldn't remember what Holly looked like. I saw Paz's round face instead, but with Holly's blond hair. Once Daddy Jake said that loving too many people in your life is like having a bowling alley inside your head.

The bus stopped at the Shell station. Everything looked the same. Kickers were pumping gas into their dented pick-ups, as usual. It was so weird. You could live another whole life that changed you forever, yet when you came back, everyone was doing the same thing as before. But maybe *they* had changed, too.

I turned up Willow and walked real slow past Chloe's old house. I paused and looked at her bedroom window. She used to have French lace curtains over the window seat where she kept her stuffed lions. I could almost hear her voice. "There are so many ditzes out there, Liza! No one's as fun as you!"

"Heart/heart," I whispered.

I started counting my steps from her front walk. I could see our house. One hundred and fifty-seven. Dad's car wasn't in the driveway. I was glad because I wanted to have time alone.

The sycamore tree in the front yard seemed bigger. Holly's swing was gone. Dad still hadn't finished painting the house. Mom had given up on that years ago. He'd covered all the nails with dabs of blue paint and then quit. Once Holly had said that her dotted Swiss Easter dress matched our house.

I climbed the stairs to the porch and looked under the marigold pot for the key. Still there. Then I heard Nacho. I couldn't get the key in fast enough. He was on the other side of the door, yipping like crazy. "It's okay," I said. "I'm home!"

The key turned, and I was.

chapter 17

Nacho's stubby tail whipped around. He slobbered and licked my cheeks. When I put him down, his toenails made clicking sounds on the front hall tile. Dad had bought him a new collar, red. Better than the old one.

I followed Nacho into the kitchen, where everything was sparkling. Dad probably hadn't eaten one real meal since we'd left, just undercooked TV dinners. Once Holly had told him he should just suck on them frozen, like Popsicles.

I checked the refrigerator. Coke, beer, and eggs.

I headed upstairs to my room. Nacho leaped along beside me. My walls were repainted blue, sequin blue, almost the color of the Rockport bay.

I heard Dad's car pulling in the driveway, but I kept sitting on my bed, holding Nacho. It didn't feel like my room exactly, but it was the best blue I'd seen.

When I went downstairs, Dad was already in the kitchen, peering into the freezer.

"Hi," I said.

He turned and smiled. Then he hugged me. I could tell if I grew one more inch, I'd be taller than he was. "I've missed my girl," he said. "Your mother called and said you were on your way. Said you had a rough time with Chloe. I'm so sorry. Are you okay? She said you made an awful lot of sacrifices this summer."

"She said that?"

"She also had some amazing news. Now Mama Lacy is saying she wants to move into Moonhaven with Daddy Jake."

"She *wants* to?" I remembered the greeting I'd sent with Mama Lacy's roses. "Número Uno, always. Jake."

Dad sighed. "Your mother can give you details. It's beyond me. I'm just so glad you're home."

Home. Forrest! The Willow Street pool. The roof. I knelt and buried my face in Nacho's fur. Then I picked up his long ear and whispered, "Summer's over."

I thought about summer. I remembered how the lights on the pier had reflected in the water like tiny stars. I remembered wading into the bay with Chloe, the mud on the bottom oozing like oatmeal between our toes.

Dad was still talking. ". . . I don't have a clue. I don't

quite believe it yet, but Mama Lacy's saying it's time to be with Jake. Of course, if they run out of pork at Moonhaven, she might change her mind. Few things last forever. Go call your mother. Let her know you're all right.''

I called Rockport. I'd wait to call Forrest until I was all alone. Or maybe I'd just show up at his door.

"Darling?" Mom said.

"I'm home.''

"Good.'' She sighed. "Where you belong! Did your father tell you the news? Mama said she'd decided she couldn't stand the thought of you going to these Rockport schools. She said, 'Liza needs to stay in San Antonio because a brain like hers deserves the best education.' ''

"A brain like mine? She said that?'' Mama Lacy had decided to leave her house on Raht Street because of me.

"I suppose it didn't hurt that Daddy wooed her with all the flowers and candy either. Anyway, she's decided on Moonhaven, at least for now.''

"Don Juan lives!" I said. "When are you coming?''

"Thanks for asking. Once I get Mama settled, I'll bring your things with me, darling. I can't wait to have our family together again.''

Together again. I hesitated. All year I'd wanted to ask. Now was the time. "Where are Holly's ashes?''

She was quiet. I could hear her breathing.

"Holly's urn is in my closet there in San Antonio," she said, "inside the hatbox."

"The *hatbox?*"

She didn't answer for a long moment. Then she said, "Darling, I couldn't bear to part with them. We thought of having the ashes sprinkled on the water down here in Rockport. That's what Mama wanted. But your father wanted to keep the urn on the mantel in San Antonio next to Holly's photo. I just couldn't think about it then, so I put the urn in the hatbox."

I thought about Holly inside the dark hatbox inside the dark closet.

"Liza, are you there?" Mom said.

"I'm here."

"Are you all right?"

"Yes," I said. I didn't feel mad anymore. I just wanted to get Holly out of the dark. "Mom?" I said.

"Hmm?"

"Sometimes I talk to her," I said. "Like a confab."

She didn't answer at first. Then she said, "So do I."

We were quiet. Finally she said, "Now I think your father's right. Holly's urn belongs on our mantel." Her voice sounded strong. "Liza?" she said. "Your grandmother wants to speak to you. Good night, darling."

The volleyball voice blasted my ear. "Liza? Are you all right?"

"Yes. Are you?"

She laughed. "Suppose you could say so. Jake's happy. I'll keep you posted."

"Could you do me a favor, Mama Lacy? I didn't say good-bye to Jennifer. Could you call and tell her that I never got around to writing that editorial for her newsletter? Tell her I'll E-mail her."

Mama Lacy said she would.

Then we said good night.

□

The clock struck nine while I was talking to Mom. That was always Holly's bedtime, an hour before mine.

"I'm going for chocolate doughnut holes," Dad said. "Make us some cocoa, would you?" He reached for the car keys and hugged me before he left.

I headed for Mom's closet and found the hatbox in the far corner. I carried it to the kitchen. Nacho followed.

The fluorescent light glared as I placed the pink hatbox on the counter and took off the lid. Wrapped in tissue was a silver jar shaped like a big sugar bowl. Mom had called it an urn. I placed it on the counter, rubbed some smudges off with my fingers, then stood back to look at the baby roses etched into the silver.

Holly was inside. We were alone together. Finally.

"It's not a bad urn, Holl," I said. "It's prettier than any casket."

The fluorescent bulb above us flickered as if it were about to go out. The clock in the hall chimed.

"It's late, Holly," I said. "Dad will be back any minute with doughnut holes. Chocolate."

I picked at the tape that sealed the urn's lid. I hoped it was sealed tight, maybe glued forever. But the tape peeled right off. I knew I could stop if I wanted. Put the tape back on again. Just not look inside.

But I had to. I had to see. I ran my fingers over the etched roses on the urn. Then I took the lid off.

I'd expected to see only dusty stuff but I saw some tiny splinters. The light flickered overhead. Nacho whined. I reached inside and picked out one tiny splinter. I held it in my palm. It was about the size of a splinter I got in my finger once from the porch railing. I kept the splinter out when I resealed the urn with new Scotch tape. I went to the living room and placed the urn on the mantel beside the photo of Holly in her pink leotard.

Then I told Nacho I was going outside. He got really excited because he thought we were going for a walk.

"You're staying here," I said. I had to hurry.

I got the trowel and my flashlight. Then I went outside with Holly's splinter in my hand.

The yard was blaring with crickets, and the sky was splattered with stars. When I was little, I thought the sky was a round dome over Willow Street, like the Astrodome. I figured you had to punch holes in the dome, like portholes, to crawl into outer space. I thought every star was a porthole.

Now I knelt under the sycamore tree where I'd buried the tip of Mama Lacy's finger. Holly's swing used to hang right above. I dug a small hole, then shone the flashlight on the splinter in my palm. It looked like a tiny, tiny wishbone.

On Thanksgiving Holly and I had always pulled on the wishbone together. She could never keep her wishes secret. On our last Thanksgiving together she'd told me her wish was to be the first woman to walk on the moon.

Now I looked up. The moon was almost full. Maybe Holly was up there walking around on it. She could be. She could be anywhere. If part of Holly was in the urn, and if her wishbone was planted beside Mama Lacy's fingertip, then why couldn't part of her be on the moon?

I heard Dad's car. He was back with our doughnuts. I looked up through the sycamore leaves at the sky. Then I dropped her splinter into the tiny grave, covered it, and turned off my flashlight.